N...
H...

by A...

comes to lite
on the movie screen

starring
KEIR DULLEA · SUSAN PENHALIGON

11 - 14 - 77

(12)

D0547296

*Leopard
in the
Snow*

Guest Stars
KENNETH MORE · BILLIE WHITELAW

featuring GORDON THOMSON as MICHAEL
and JEREMY KEMP as BOLT

Produced by JOHN QUESTED and CHRIS HARROP
Screenplay by ANNE MATHER and JILL HYEM
Directed by GERRY O'HARA
An Anglo-Canadian Co-Production

OTHER
Harlequin Romances
by MARGARET WAY

Many of these titles are available at your local bookseller
or through the Harlequin Reader Service.

For a free catalogue listing all available Harlequin Romances,
send your name and address to:

HARLEQUIN READER SERVICE,
M.P.O. Box 707, Niagara Falls, N.Y. 14302
Canadian address: Stratford, Ontario, Canada N5A 6W4

or use order coupon at back of books.

Black Ingo

by

MARGARET WAY

Harlequin Books

TORONTO • LONDON • NEW YORK • AMSTERDAM • SYDNEY

Original hardcover edition published in 1977
by Mills & Boon Limited

ISBN 0-373-02132-1

Harlequin edition published January 1978

PRINTED IN U.S.A.

CHAPTER ONE

FELICITY RUSSELL put her empty glass down and hoisted her slipping glasses from the bridge of her small, pretty nose.

'A love affair may cause me worries!' she read avidly. 'How fascinating!'

'No chance of that on Tandarro!' Genny said dryly, thanking her lucky stars.

'If only Ingo weren't my cousin!' Felicity moaned, regretful but resigned, picking up where she left off on her horoscope. She took it all very seriously, the excitements and the difficulties, the important decisions that had to be held off. At thirty-nine, nearing forty, Felicity was a celebrated beauty, dreamy and fragile to the point of frailty, with a miraculous and seemingly indestructible look of the lovely blooming twenties, and very little else to disprove the traditional theory about blondes. Scatty she might have been, but she was very likeable, totally without malice and irresistible to the male of the species since she had given her first little breathy hiccough. The doctor at that time had no other choice but to pronounce her the prettiest baby he had ever delivered when in fact she was just that.

Genuinely foolish mother, didn't wish to pursue that line of thought. Her mother's love affairs, deliciously exciting as they were to her, had caused no end of trouble. Felicity, all her life, had just sat back and let people look after her and fall in love with her. First her family and their many relations, then her three husbands—two divorced, one Genny's father who had

5

named her Giannina, and the last who had left Felicity a respectable widow, saving Genny lots of additional embarrassment at school. Felicity might gladden the eye but she very often left the heart aching, and knowing that had built up certain deep tensions in Genny. She was the man of the house. It sounded odd, but that was how she thought of herself. The Protector.

Felicity was glancing up into her daughter's eyes, her rosebud mouth pouting. 'Now Ingo, there's a man!'

'He thinks you're a perfect fool!' Genny said sharply.

'Darling!' her mother broke off from her musing. 'How nasty, and how unlike you.'

'You know what I mean!' Genny shrugged her shoulders. 'Ingo Faulkner thinks all women are fools.'

'You're much too hard on him.'

'Isn't he hard on me?' Genny challenged. 'What was it he called me the last time? That crazy revved-up kid. Not even to my face either. Big deal. I only took his wretched horse.'

'It did throw you, the great brute!'

'Just a little tumble, I wasn't hurt. Anyway, it's a beautiful animal,' sighed Genny. 'It's Ingo I loathe. The more I see of him, the more I want to kick him hard on the shins.'

'Now that is childish, but I know what you mean, he's so *physical*. Remember he's your cousin too, darling.'

'Correction, he's *your* cousin. Your second cousin, actually. I take after my father.'

'Dear God!' Felicity's small face is . . . . distinctly pained. 'Must you remind me of him?'

'You could have kept him if you wanted him.'

'Honestly, darling, if you start that again I shall get up and go. It wasn't all bad, I'll admit. All the Italians are madly passionate. Carlo loved me, cherished me. He was frantically in love with me but so jealous, you can't imagine. It really takes hold of some people and it's so *wearing*. The only slight peace I got was when I was carrying you. He was charming then, when I wasn't even presentable. I suppose he could afford to turn a blind eye. Anyway, I've quite forgiven him. You have his beautiful dark eyes and my silver curls—it's really wildly effective.'

'It must be, if it persuaded you to try contact lenses.'

'That was just a little joke!' Felicity waved her hand. 'I've done quite all right with my own blue eyes.'

'Oh, I know you have!' Genny said violently. 'No wonder I've always acted the ghastly little horror, and it was mostly an act. I had to drive them off some way.'

'My brave little girl!' Felicity said fondly, her eyes sparkling with real tears. Genny had indeed been quite thorough in her intentions and at an extremely tender age. 'And a bluestocking too!' Felicity said, still greatly surprised.

'No one says bluestocking any more, Flick!' reproved Genny.

'*I* do. I can't get over it in a daughter of mine. Of course Carlo had a lot of education, it's necessary for men. Why aren't you romantic, darling? You should be. What else is a woman born for if not for great romances? All this interest in study disturbs me. I was quite stupid at school, would you believe? I'd lose heart entirely, only you've inherited my beauty!'

'I don't look very much like you.'

Felicity smiled. 'You're too close to me to see it, darling. Others remark on it. Of course you have a look of your dear father and that gorgeous pale olive skin. I've always had to keep out of the sun myself. Just a frail little flower with a lifetime in the shade.'

'Then why go to Tandarro? Goodness knows the sun glitters down there. I've never seen such light.'

'Tandarro is a wonderful place, you know that. My family are proud of their cattle kings!'

'Black Ingo!' mocked Genny.

'Don't harp on that—and don't let him catch you calling him that.'

'He already has!'

'You're not very clever with Ingo,' Felicity said quite seriously.

'Really?' Genny said sarcastically, but she smiled.

'Why, Ingo—dear me, dear me, I can't think of a finer, stronger man.'

'For that matter neither can I. I just hate him.'

'Well, he doesn't hate you,' Felicity said resolutely. 'Indeed, he was greatly taken with you as a child. All those conversations you had! I can scarcely believe all the unspeakable things you say about one another now. Even if we weren't beholders to him I don't like you calling him names, and Tandarro is a haven of peace and beauty. I shall grow strong again. We should be very grateful to Ingo for letting us come.'

Genny turned her face away, swallowing an involuntary exclamation. Maybe Ingo put her in perpetual revolt, but he was her mother's cousin and, she had to admit, a true friend. No one could make an enemy of Felicity anyway. She was so vague she wouldn't even recognise one.

'To think that in a few days we'll be there!' Felicity was enthusing. 'Thank you again, darling, for saying you'd come with me. I know you wanted to go off to Bali in the uni vacation!'

'I guess I did!' Genny emitted a jagged breath. 'But the doctor said you needed care. That was a bad virus. You're such a slip of a thing it's hard to realise you're anyone's mother.'

'Oh, Carlo decided that, I didn't. Of course, darling, I adore you and I did from the moment you arrived, but it didn't start off that way. I was very delicate as a child. I know you make a joke of it and I know you

8

don't like to frighten me, but I must be treated as something precious. Why, you're as wonderful to me as my own Mamma, God rest her soul.'

'Don't I know it!' Genny said dryly. 'I'm convinced you'd perish without me.'

'Pretty much, darling. Would you refill my glass?'

'That's it! Just the one.'

Felicity stared at her and Genny relented slightly. 'All right, half way. I'm glad you're looking forward to Ingo's company.'

'He's been very good to me,' Felicity sighed, never for one moment mentioning just how good, or the fact Ingo had virtually supported them since poor Hughie died without leaving them secure. Hughie Russell's posthumous financial standing had come as a severe shock to Felicity. They had always lived very well, and Hughie had been the last man in the world to deny her anything. No doubt all his efforts on her behalf had brought about his untimely demise. Of course he had been twenty years older, but much too young and dapper to die. She had never loved him, of course. For the first time in her life Felicity had used her head when she married and it hadn't worked out either. One could fare just as badly being sensible.

'I just hope I can stick it out!' Genny murmured truthfully.

'The trouble is, darling, Ingo seems to bring out the worst in you. You really do act like a young hellion sometimes. It must be the tempestuous Italian side of your nature. Even your silver curls sparkle with rage and your skin runs up red flags. I mean, he's not too bad really. Even your uneducated eye must be able to see he's wildly attractive!'

'Yes, he looks just like a movie star,' replied Genny.

'Nothing as silly as that, dear. He's a cattle man. It's his whole life, running a great station. I know he can

9

take a very hard line, but the odd thing is that when he puts himself out, he could charm the birds off the trees. He can charm little ole me!'

'Then I suppose we'd better thank God he's your cousin and he definitely thinks of you as *family*. An appendage. Responsibility.'

'I dig you, darling,' said Felicity. 'Really you're funny sometimes!'

'You've made me funny. It's not easy having an enchantress for a mother.'

'I'm not a patch on you, darling, and I never was, not even when Carlo made off with me.'

Genny threw back her shining head and gave a lilting little laugh. 'I can't accept that. That's mother-love talking.'

'I can't help feeling that neither of us has any vanity.'

'For what? Gifts from the gods. Beauty can hurt.'

'It never hurt me,' Felicity said artlessly, not grasping Genny's meaning. 'But then you're so much more intelligent than I. Also, believe me, darling, and I'm not joking, more beautiful. You just haven't realised it yet.'

'It's silly to complain, but I don't think Ingo wants me out there.'

'But of course, dear, that's *impossible*! Why, Ingo's letters are full of questions about you.'

Genny rounded on her mother in astonishment, her velvety dark eyes huge. 'What letters?'

'Why, the letter the other day!' Felicity said vaguely. '*I* never saw it.'

'Hasn't anyone ever told you I'm the head of the house? At least I was on the census form!' Why, Felicity thought, if Genny knew Ingo was paying for her education it would quite drive her towards getting a job; but that was part of the bargain Ingo struck. Genny was to know nothing. Sometimes it occurred to Felicity that Ingo actually liked Genny's fiery pride. He was quick

10

and ready to take her to task, but he was really the only male discipline Genny had known. Carlo, the great passion of Felicity's life but nevertheless a traitor, had gone back to Italy after Felicity had left him, threatening to blow his brains out. As it happened he decided to remain on the green earth, and indulged himself in another marriage with a fellow countrywoman. The woods were full of women, as Ingo had pointed out then. Even beautiful women. He had been pretty cynical even then. Just a handsome boy with a stepmother he detested but who definitely didn't detest him.

At twenty-three, a divorcee, Felicity had been left rejoicing in a ravishingly pretty little daughter with her father's thickly-lashed melting dark eyes and the faint dimple in her chin, and had remarried yet another unsuitable type, though his ancestors hailed from the Scottish Highlands; almost a double for Carlo. But even Felicity learned something from both experiences, for when she married again in her mid-thirties she chose a man with infinitely fewer physical endowments than either Carlo or Stewart and a great deal more stability. Hughie had been a fine man and she had treated him with such sweetness and genuine affection that he had never been aware she had never loved him. It was all very sad, because Hughie had shown Genny the same loving indulgence he would have extended to his own daughter. The one marriage that might have worked out, and he had died on her! Could it be she was destined to dazzle men, then destroy them? The thought often kept Felicity luxuriously unhappy.

'Where have you gone off to, Flick?' Genny asked tenderly, admiring her mother's quickly changing, all oming expressions.

'as thinking about Hughie.'

'old Hughie, bless his heart. Even Ingo approf him, and that takes some doing.'

11

'I made him happy, didn't I, darling?'

Genny grinned. 'Indeed you did. Hughie couldn't have been happier married to Helen of Troy.'

'You say the nicest things sometimes. I didn't have to expend myself on Hughie. I'm so frail. When I remember that brute strength of Carlo's!'

'That's going back a bit—I'm twenty years old.'

'We were talking of your father,' reproved Felicity. 'There's no need to establish your age or mine.'

'Well, where we're going we won't be able to hide anything! They've known us too long. Black Ingo used to dandle me on his knee. I must have worn him down; he only wants to turn me over it now.'

'Small wonder!' Felicity sniffed her small fastidious nose. 'I don't know what either of you are trying to prove, but I want you to behave yourself better this time.'

'Never simple with Ingo around. He goes out of his way to provoke me.'

'To a certain degree I have to admit that's true. Perhaps you both require a character analysis. I know I frequently remind you and you don't like it, but he did save your life.'

'Then there's no need for him to act as if that's what he was put on this earth for!' snapped Genny.

'I feel sick every time I think of it!' Felicity moaned, transported back over the years to a time when the small, high-spirited Genny had run straight in front of a galloping horse. Ingo, the only one not frozen with shock, had moved with incredible speed, gathering her up and flinging them both to safety. Genny had been tremendously attached to him then, clinging to him for the rest of the day. It was ridiculous really the they argued now. The rebellious instincts in G were being fed and kept alive by Ingo's positiv dominance, and the conflict that had been brou

12

by Genny's adolescence seemed destined to go on. It almost cast a shadow on Felicity's feeling of contentment. Genny was stuck in a groove about Ingo, but Felicity felt the familiar rush of pleasure at the thought of seeing him again.

Ingo regarded her with some amusement, she knew, thinking her a frantic butterfly forever attracted towards disaster, which perhaps explained the rather stern line he took with Genny; but Felicity knew, with a mixture of pride and thankfulness, that he regarded them both as special and his inevitable responsibility. Felicity even fancied they touched his heart from time to time, which wasn't all that easy. Ingo, though born to wealth and position and a fine respected name, had been caught in some pretty fierce battles between his parents from his earliest years. The story was familiar. Marianne, his mother, an alien in the vast desert wilderness with only the homestead as a mere pinprick of civilisation, had just got up one morning after twelve years of marriage and decided she could stand the loneliness and the isolation no longer. She had gathered up her son and her daughter and fled Tandarro without stopping, but Marc had caught up with her. A hard and ruthless man when he had to be, Marc had demanded his son, but extended some mercy to Marianne in allowing her to keep their daughter, Patricia. The girl had stayed with her mother.

Ingo had been taken back to the station and reared by his aunt Evelyn, a veritable dragon to Felicity's way of thinking. Later, Ingo came by a stepmother, a woman he knew for what she was the moment he laid eyes on her. No one could ever take his mother's place and no one ever tried. So Ingo had grown up a singularly self-reliant young man with indomitable strength and endurance but nothing to give to any woman. It was melancholy, Felicity often considered, for Ingo was a marvellous human being with a perversely strong attraction for the sex he professed to despise. His grey eyes, the ultimate blaze of light in his intensely self-contained face, darkly tanned by the sun, his sardonic, vaguely disdainful manner, were quite hypnotic.

Felicity had often witnessed Ingo's turbulent effect on women. That hard, inaccessible look, the smiling look of contempt in his shining pewter-grey eyes, seemed to draw them like moths to a lamp. Except that she really did think of him as family, Felicity might have succumbed herself. Superb arrogance like that got a woman every time. Only Genny was reserved from that quality of cynicism never far from his eyes. Her recurring defiant stances earned some pretty grim words, far more than she asked for, Felicity often thought, but the funny thing was that Ingo was completely involved and far from indifferent to the stormy child Genny often seemed to be, bent rather recklessly on disobeying not just any but all of the Boss's orders—a kind of rebellion unheard-of on Tandarro where no one would think of anything so foolish or ill-advised.

Genny, every year since she was about fourteen, had become more and more restless and self-assertive in Ingo's presence. The adorable little-girl stage had passed when Ingo had been a very willing hero. Now they were antagonists animated by any number of arguments. The previous beautiful communication had degenerated into heated exchanges and an occasional brilliant smile from one or the other that had a strange power to set everything right until the next time. Whatever place Genny held in Ingo's mind she was securely entrenched in his life and his formidable list of responsibilities. The bright, bitter-sweet, intolerable little running battles he probably gave no more thought to than as a young girl's heady bid for equality and independence.

However conveniently he managed to hide it from her, Ingo wrote and spoke of Genny as someone special. It was useless to fight him, even if Genny showed a considerable amount of initiative doing it. Neither, Felicity suspected, hated their battles as much as they made out. Perhaps it was some weird kind of game between them, for Ingo had shown time and time again that he understood Genny better than she understood herself, and this remarkable knowledge perhaps made Genny a captive. One couldn't sit around looking self-absorbed and mysterious with Ingo, his tall frame just swooped with absurd speed to return one to reality. One could never hope for the quiet life with Ingo about. Something was always happening. Even so, Felicity knew there was no place she wished to be for some time to come rather than Tandarro, where she was waited on hand and foot like a visiting queen. It was most agreeable and naturally a bad virus had made her extremely cautious about her health. Rheumatic fever as a child had complicated her life, pretty nearly everyone treated her like Imperial porcelain. It was a great blessing that Ingo was so rich and so generous.

Felicity could never, and understandably never, have worked for a living. When she felt much better, at some time in the future, she would try to get hold of some other good man like Hughie Russell, but younger, with a more presentable bank balance. A woman was nothing without a man and it was no use for Genny in her youthful ignorance to harp about independence and how it made the heart glad. Only being loved made Felicity come alive. She needed kisses and caresses and constant courting as a baby needed regular feeding. A work of art, she was born to be admired and looked after in luxury. Other women might be committed to housework and putting out a sparkling wash; Felicity had done very well in avoiding both. A cleaning lady called twice a week and Genny kept a good supply of rubber gloves to protect her hands while cleaning the place in between. It was perfectly well known that Felicity wasn't strong enough to embrace any more arduous task than arranging the flowers, which she did with a great deal of magic.

Genny's softly chiding voice brought Felicity back to the immediate present. 'Sorry, darling, did I go off again?' she asked in a slightly dazed fashion.

'Yes, that's right.'

'I'm sorry. My mind just oscillates round so many subjects. I think so clearly about so many things, so many people. I never have time to be bored.' Felicity took a sip from her long frosted glass, made an appreciative little moue, then leaned back in her reclining chair and crossed her slender legs at the ankle, glancing down with habitual pleasure. 'It's great not having to diet to keep so slender. All my family were thoroughbreds, built for speed.'

'Well, I've heard you called fast,' teased Genny.

'I married every one of them.'

Genny shook her head. Felicity had to. Carlo and Stewart and Hughie had lots of company. Admirers had always streamed around her mother's feet. 'Is Ingo coming for us?' she asked with remarkable crispness.

'Really, Genny, you know he's too busy at this time. We're to take the charter flight to Warrego and he'll pick us up there.'

'Do you actually want to go that badly?'

'Darling, at this point there's nowhere I'd rather go. I love Tandarro. It's so weirdly beautiful. The contrast between the homestead and its bizarre setting is enough to make the mind flutter. We should have plenty of company as well, what with the holiday season and Christmas coming up. Trish and the children are coming, did I tell you?'

'As a matter of fact you didn't. You're unwontedly silent about Ingo's communications!'

'I feel I have to be, as a lot of them are about you.'

Genny snorted. 'Amazing! At a distance he cares for me. At close range he's the damnedest man in the world. Black Ingo, the untameable. I think I'm even a little afraid of him.'

'I don't think he would care to hear himself described that way. Black as in what? A black heart? A black soul?'

'Neither,' Genny said, her silver-gilt head turned away. 'Black as in tortuous. Deep. Complicated. Unknowable. I run out of words with Ingo.'

Her mother regarded her for some little time. 'Really? That wasn't my impression, not now or at any other time. You've quite a tongue on you. You call him Black Ingo—I call him cousin. He's a jewel.'

'His eyes are like jewels.'

'Indeed!' said Felicity. 'I've seen any number of women work up a grand passion for Ingo, including his stepmamma!'

'How nice that we don't see her any more. Actually I think Ingo was rather cruel to her.'

'He was in a good position to *feel* cruel!' Felicity said firmly. 'She was a bitch through and through. Marc would never have married her, only he was so bitter and disillusioned about Marianne. Ingo has suffered in his way. He was only ten or so when Marianne left, and I know he considered himself abandoned by the mother he adored. There was no one closer to Marc's heart than Ingo, but of course Marc couldn't express himself in that way. Old man Faulkner, the grandfather, was becote an eccentric. He brought them all up, Marc and
'I wand Evelyn, in military fashion. It affected every
'Poor them, and then again he never approved of proved

Marianne. Beautiful and well-connected she might have been, but she was city bred, and the land for its own sake never interested her. Tandarro always got in the way. It must have been very difficult for her. Poor Marianne!'

'There's such a thing as putting things right!' Genny maintained passionately. 'Why won't Ingo see his mother? He allows Trish and her family to come.'

'Trish is his sister. Remember she suffered as Ingo did. Children have no part to play in adult situations; Trish was heartbroken to be parted from Ingo.'

'Yet their parents allowed it.'

'They couldn't stay together, Genny. Remember the old man was actively hostile towards Marianne and they had to live in his home until he died. Neither Marc nor any one of them would ever have left Tandarro, so Marianne had to go. Ingo, as heir to a great heritage, necessarily had to stay with his father. God knows he loves the place as much as even his grandfather wanted. He's never forgiven his mother, you know.'

'Don't I know it,' agreed Genny. 'Every inch of him, six feet and over, rejects a woman's integrity. He's so uncompromising. Then he can be so damned, so damned . . .'

'. . . charming . . . ?'

'So damned *Ingo*, he makes such a claim on you, you can't turn away from him. He's simply an enigma.'

'And you can't hold your own with him.'

'I try.'

Felicity sat up and tilted her swanlike neck. 'You usually start everything. Why must you always be so daring? I know Ingo enjoys a lot of it, but he's not a man to trifle with, darling. Why don't you promote a wonderful new relationship or go back to the unremitting bliss of childhood? You won him effortlessly then.

I can still see you. Such an enchanting child you were, with those radiant silver curls and poor impossible Carlo's velvet eyes. Is it any wonder Ingo called you Cherub?'

'He surely doesn't now!'

'That's your fault. You resist him so strenuously. Why don't you take a leaf out of my book?'

'Oh, nothing so combustible!' Genny said, and smiled. 'I mightn't be anything like you, with the soft dazzlement, but I don't mind!'

'Then don't turn Tandarro into a battlefield between you. You've got my cameo face—it should mean something. I know you can be sweet as run honey when you want to be. Didn't the immensely arrogant Ingo allow you to invite all your intellectual friends for a golden month on Tandarro?'

'He won't be caught with that one again.'

Felicity began to laugh. 'Do you blame him? That silly Perry girl couldn't be sidetracked from his side.'

Genny shrugged. 'She's quite intelligent really, just particularly smitten with Ingo, heaven knows why.'

'Oh, come on now,' Felicity jeered, visibly reacting, 'Let's not kid ourselves, Ingo is terrific! A cattle baron. A power . . .'

'The iron fist without the velvet glove.'

'Every other female but you seems to go dreamy about him,' her mother told her.

'I know him too well.'

'You don't know him at all!'

'If I thought I'd be really frightened.' Genny reached her arms above her head and stretched. 'Will Evelyn be there?'

'Regrettably, yes. He couldn't very well throw her out like Barbara. Still, she keeps out of the way a lot!'

'True. She hasn't had much of a life.'

'I believe she had an admirer at one time,' said

Felicity, 'but Evelyn was always too proud to be practical. No one ever measured up to her father and brothers!'

'What she was, and is, they made of her. Implacable sort of men, very sure of themselves. I've never minded poor old Evvy. She never had a chance for all she was Miss Evelyn Faulkner of Tandarro. She had no rights; the Faulkner men have had all the rights. Big, handsome, arrogant devils!'

'I'm all for them,' said Felicity, and Genny scowled.

'I'm not. In fact, I'm coming more and more to a whole new outlook on men and marriage. The image of woman is changing, but it's still a man's world. Take the life on the land, the man is all-powerful. His physical strength alone makes his the vital role. He has the danger and the excitement and the mateship. Women aren't really wanted except to look after the house and look pretty, if possible.'

'That applies just about everywhere. What's wrong with looking pretty anyway?'

'I hope to God I'm more than a pretty face. I'm a mind! I have a significant, important role to play. I love children and I want them eventually, but I don't want to be limited to just a single role. I'm a whole person and I want to be accepted as just that in this male-dominated world.'

'You mean you want to be Ingo's equal?' asked Felicity.

'Is anyone Ingo's equal?'

'If I were you I'd settle for being a woman on a pedestal. It never did me any harm.'

'We have different natures. It would be hard to get close to a really dominant man,' argued Genny.

'That's unarguable. Marianna certainly didn't. She was very sensitive, but she wasn't a weak woman. She simply wore herself out in a desperate effort to survive scale. Tandarro, the Faulkners' rightful place in the sun! An heir must be assured whether Ingo likes it or not.'

'Well, darling, he mightn't trust us all that much, but he hasn't been without consolation all these years.'

'Just never suffered embarrassing consequences. Ingo knows how to take good care of himself.'

'He's extremely self-sufficient, yes. Why are you always wanting to change him?'

'I don't know,' Genny muttered, apparently to herself. 'Who told you about Sally?'

'Trix.'

'Ah, Trix, her ears are always patrolling. She must never go off duty.'

'Trix is all right. What else do you expect her to do?'

'Go for a walk. Get a job. Anything.'

'With *that* money? I wish to God that Hughie ...' Felicity broke off.

'Yes, continue,' Genny invited in the sudden silence. 'What about Hughie?'

'Nothing,' Felicity said, and shrugged her delicate shoulders.

'You gave me to understand that Hughie left us quite comfortable,' insisted Genny.

'So he did, but you mustn't confuse Hughie's money with the McFarlane fortunes. Trix must be one of the richest women in the country,' Felicity added fast. Now at this late date she didn't start any discussion on the true source of their income. Genny knew that Ingo presented them with a fat cheque from time to time; what she didn't know was that that was a glorious bonus with the monthly cheques undetected. 'Think you can do without Dave for a while?' Felicity tacked on by way of a further red herring.

'Dave's just a friend!' Genny answered, continuing to search her mother's lovely sky-blue eyes.

'I wish you'd at least be normal!' Felicity sighed. 'Dave is in love with you.'

'How nice!'

'Doesn't that mean something?' Felicity implored. 'He's so attractive and he comes from such a good family, and I like him.'

'You like any male who knows how to butter you up. Dave is pretty fond of you too.'

'I know, and he's *suffering*, darling. Why don't you put him out of his agony?'

Genny's dark eyes were grave, her eyebrows like delicate wings rising. 'I never know what you're talking about. You surely can't mean promise to marry him?'

'Why not? At least get engaged.'

'Flick, you're quite mad!' Genny said solemnly. 'I'm too young to get married even if I loved Dave, which I don't.'

'At your age I was a mother!' Felicity announced with sudden tremendous feeling.

'You have to take the good with the bad,' Genny murmured laconically.

'I really feel sorry for Dave. Every mother wants a doctor in the family.'

'That's your idea, Flick. I like Dave. More, I'm pleasantly interested in him, but I don't think I love him, whatever that means. If he went off to South America to study tropical diseases I'd just buy him a pair of gumboots in a fairly good frame of mind. I can do without him, that's the point.'

'You're foolish to let him get away, darling,' Felicity admonished. 'You're practically settled yourself. You're such a brain I'm sure you've flown through your finals.'

'I want to get my Dip. Ed.,' Genny said doggedly.

'But why, darling?' Felicity fluttered her small, innocent-of-toil hands. 'Young girls are so different these days—all this emphasis on the brain! I'm quite sure it will hurt you. I mean, the side effects remain to be seen. You're far and away the prettiest girl in your set, yet you're so aloof I wonder Dave dares kiss you.'

'Oh, he does,' Genny said dryly. 'I like it too, but nothing unusual happens. No stars gyrate, no bells ring out. I like Dave and I admire him. He's fun, he's very quick and intelligent. I guess it adds up to the fact that the man one can like is not the man one can love. Love must be pretty potent stuff, otherwise all the great writers are having us on. Maybe it just exists between pages. On the other hand, I can't help feeling a grand passion would frighten me a little.'

'Luckily it never frightened me!' Felicity said complacently.

'No, you seem to be able to stand enormous amounts of punishment, Flick.'

'Not punishment, darling. Women love to suffer.'

'You're joking!'

'No, I'm not. If we were really suffering the way we pretended, of course we'd be killed right away. It's just a momentous game. One can always turn a corner and find a new love.'

'That doesn't seem sensible!' Genny said, looking back on her mother's immeasurable romances. 'And I don't think I'd want that sort of thing.'

'Don't I know it!' Felicity deplored. 'In that respect you're not even Carlo's daughter. Anyway, I suppose it helped you get through your studies. Ask Dave out to Tandarro, I'm sure Ingo wouldn't mind. When you smile you can twist even Ingo around your little finger.'

'Wouldn't I love to do it!' Genny said, her eyes narrowing.

'Oh, why?'

'It would be quite an achievement. Ingo isn't like Dave. Dave's just a boy.'

24

'Ingo's only six or seven years older,' Felicity pointed out.

'Oh, Ingo's tremendously mature. He's the mocking observer who stands way back looking down his straight nose at all of us. Ingo won't lose himself in a mad passion. He's brilliant, a man apart. Oh yes, he'll amuse himself briefly and shatter a few dreams, but he won't abandon himself to any woman. He just likes to smile at them contemptuously with those shining light eyes.'

Felicity was sitting up, an expression of surprise on her face. 'You're most acutely aware of Ingo, aren't you? I've never really paid any attention before. I mean, man-woman aware. You must be growing up. If it didn't sound so ridiculous I'd say you were halfway in love with him and you have been these many years.'

Genny almost stuttered in her sudden rage. 'Are you crazy?'

'I really don't know,' her mother teased. 'You ask it a lot!'

'Lordy, Flick!'

'There you go again, sparking away like blazes. Only one person I know sets you off, Ingo. As I said, he's just beautiful, that unassailable creature. If Ingo kissed you, you'd see a few stars. Summer lightning as well!'

'Stop smirking, Flick. He's not going to bother either of us!' With her colour up and her dark eyes stormy Genny had such a beauty, such a strong echo of Carlo, that Felicity closed her eyes as though warding off a vision.

'I bet Sally will land herself an invitation.'

'Good luck to her!' Genny said, managing to sound just the opposite.

'I like Sally!' Felicity said, not altogether truthfully.

'She tries too hard!' Genny maintained. 'I'd like to tell her it's a mistake being nice to Ingo. She ought to give him a little of his own medicine.'

25

'She'd be ill for days! Do invite Dave out. He's great company, and he's so attentive he makes me feel so young again.'

'You *are* young,' smiled Genny. 'You'll always be young. You're my mother and I love you, you juvenile delinquent!'

'Thank you, darling. I know you're the wise one.'

'I'd better wait and ask Ingo first.'

'Oh, don't be silly, I'm sure he won't mind. He expects it. Tandarro could comfortably house an army, let alone feed one. I've told him about Dave, as a matter of fact.'

'You've told him *what*?' Genny reached out and scooped up a handful of her mother's hair. 'Surely there's nothing to tell!'

Felicity hit Genny's hand away. 'Remember when you were late getting back from Hastings? Dave spoke his piece then. It nearly brought tears to my eyes. He wants to marry you, Genny. He's very serious and he's very practical. He has lots of plans—I like that. All my plans fall apart at the seams.'

'And you told Ingo this?'

'I'm not dumb. Ingo likes to know everything. Such a thing he might consider important. You know, give the bride away and that sort of thing.'

'What did he say?' Genny demanded.

'As a matter of fact,' Felicity said, looking away, 'it wasn't complimentary.'

'Did you imagine he would be happy for me?'

'He thinks you need a strong hand.'

Genny shrugged. 'Dave certainly hasn't got one. The woman who marries Dave had better be prepared to be the boss. Dave skips trouble; peace at any price.'

'I thought you liked that.'

'I did before I encountered Ingo.'

'Was there ever such a time? You were about fifteen

months old when I first took you back to Tandarro,' said Felicity.

'I don't remember.'

'Ingo does. Even as a baby he remembered a great deal. He's seen you at all the continuing stages of your development. Good or bad, there's nothing you can hide from Ingo.'

'Oh, skip it!'

'All right. I've needed to become acrobatic about my cousin—ask Dave.'

'I might. What a stroke of luck, you've provided me with a champion!'

'You've done so well with your studies I thought you deserved something,' teased Felicity. 'Now what about some new clothes? Let's go shopping tomorrow. This is a big time of the year on the property. I can't wait to get there. But of course you don't care about it!' Felicity said slyly.

'I can't really admit I love it more than you do,' said Genny moodily.

'Ingo wouldn't be surprised. You have a very transparent way of showing your feelings, and unlike me you can ride like the wind. You might at least thank him for that.'

'He seemed to blame me for it the last time.'

'The true reason was that you gave him a bad fright. Ingo doesn't normally know fear. The fall knocked you unconscious. It wasn't as though he hadn't warned you.'

'Any kind of mutiny is unsupportable with Ingo.'

'At times you really need warning,' her mother said.

'I know, I know! It was my fault. I just flattered myself I could handle the stallion and I couldn't.'

'No one but Ingo can. It's a one-rider horse. Everyone knew, and you got Jimmy into trouble. Please don't do it again. Ingo was thoroughly rattled.'

'I didn't exactly enjoy being thrown, nor the few

seconds beforehand when I could see it about to happen,' retorted Genny.

'Such courage!'

'Ingo called it suicide with his eyes flashing murder.'

'Ingo always made himself your guardian,' remembered Felicity. 'You should be very grateful for that.'

Genny clicked her tongue with real exasperation. 'So why aren't I?'

'Maybe you've been too pressured all round. You're such a conscientious child, and there's no denying Ingo can be fairly formidable when the mood takes him.'

'It would put any woman aflame, Ingo's black arrogance. Sometimes I think things will never come right between us again.'

'I don't think Ingo's exactly at ease with you, either. I mean you used to adore him, now you explode every time he says a word out of place. It's not consistent. Amazing! The two of you give me the willies!'

'Incredible to think he still wants me there. Are you sure he does? Ingo's the last man in the world I'd force myself on.'

'My darling child, will you calm yourself? Ingo insisted on you, absolutely. In his own way, however high-handed his attitude, and you do goad him. Ingo is fond of you. Take my word.' The words were uttered casually, but they conveyed utter sincerity.

Still the old pent-up antagonism was in Genny's face, her flawless young skin exquisitely tinted with colour. It didn't seem at all like her, but what she was feeling was vaguely barbaric. At more than a thousand miles away Ingo made her come out in prickly heat. The curiously blissful relationship they shared in her childhood was only an illusion. Ingo's eyes on her now made her feel over-exposed, seared to the skin. It was odd, such violence between them, and the fragments of unforgettable magic.

Tandarro had been almost a religion with her. Tandarro with its strange tribal gods and its stupendous scenery, its unpredictable seasons, its moods of upheaval, the unspeakable cruelty of drought, the spontaneous never-ending landscapes of wild flowers. Tandarro was violent, towering and tragic, filling the vision; the final inevitability was that Ingo should be so compelling. His image was always in Genny's mind, defying her to reject him.

Uncanny the way it persisted, like a sharply drawn black-and-white etching, perfect in every detail. She simply couldn't comprehend the significance of it all. Ingo, if she weakened, could turned her into anything he liked. He had an awesome drawing power, a sheer force of personality that belonged to his background. Was she simply going to walk back into his sun-dazzled kingdom, the snare of gold? It was probably very brave of her, because the danger was real. She couldn't talk about it, and it wasn't normal, but every minute she spent in Ingo's company seemed loaded. Whatever the cause, it usually goaded her into some kind of reckless action that frosted his silvery eyes. A picture of his hard, handsome face came sharply into her mind so that her tender young mouth twisted fractionally as if in some kind of pain. Ingo was a fever, and so far she hadn't found the antidote.

CHAPTER TWO

GENNY put her hand to her temples, staring up into the blazing blue sky. Her silky hair, like a silver nimbus about her head, glittered in the hot sun, but her eyes were protected by huge, round sunglasses. A few feet behind her, Felicity was reclining with beautiful languor under the only shade tree, as fresh as a bluebell in the sizzling heat. Both of them had their eyes trained on the sky, Felicity with pleasurable anticipation and a lightness of heart, Genny strung up with a queer rising perturbation. Her dark eyes behind the glasses were as intense as the set of her delicately contoured face. It was absurd, but she was feeling so aroused that her heart was hammering. All this for Ingo, when she had known him all her life! It didn't make sense, but something very like excitement lay across her, a flame that was making her blood boil.

Felicity in her green oasis looked almost a teenager in one of her chic little outfits, with a vivid blue and white bandeau bra beneath the open shirt of her pants suit. Her beautiful blonde hair had been newly cut short to flatter her small face, and her figure was as superbly taut as Genny's but without Genny's translucent golden tanned midriff. Felicity was just stunning, Genny thought with tender pride. Flower-cool, imperturbable after hours of letting Genny fend for them both. No wonder the attendant at this country airstrip had mistaken her for Genny's sister, hurrying out with a comfortable canvas chair and placing it in the shade, realising at once which young lady needed the cosseting. That kind of error was made all the time, with Felicity smiling dreamily and never once correcting. It was very pleasant to be thought a good fifteen years younger than one really was. Even sensational beauties didn't always maintain such unique preservation. Willing helpers had always been thick on the ground, and Genny was furiously efficient and methodical, prowling like a small silver cat as she waited for Ingo to arrive. Except that it was so hot, Felicity would have sprinted over to her and told her to sit down.

High up above them came the familiar drone of an engine, then the sun caught the glinting fuselage. Genny could feel the perspiration dewing her temples, curls clinging to her temples. She actually shuddered and turned back to her mother.

'Start waving, here he comes!'

'Wowee!' said Felicity, getting to her feet and whipping off her sunglasses in case they had left a mark on her nose.

The attendant came out to motion them back and all three watched the six-seater come in to land, touching down perfectly and taxiing across in front of the giant hangar.

'Right on time!' said the attendant.

'That's Ingo!' Always demonstrative, Felicity started towards the aircraft, eager for a face-to-face confrontation. Her small flying figure in her cork-heeled sandals barely skimmed the ground, as light as the willy-willy of leaves that was settling in the wake of the plane's turbulence. Genny, fearing any false move on her part, stayed well back, watching the welcoming scene unfold. It was poetic and unwillingly she had to admit it. Ingo's tall frame was silhouetted in the shimmering haze, Felicity now clinging to him like a survivor in the desert, a petite, fragile blonde, nestling against his lean powerful height.

My mother's cousin. Black Ingo. Terrific! Genny started to breathe deeply. Even at a distance he instantly struck up all kinds of tensions. His right arm was slung carelessly around Felicity's shoulders as he led her back towards her unresponsive daughter, Felicity staring up into his arresting dark face, obviously feeling cherished and sure of her welcome, anything but deprived and given to misbehaving like Genny.

'Hi, Giannina!' The light, lancing eyes briefly touched Genny's face.

31

'Hi, pal!'

'How are you coming to me, friend or foe?'

'That depends entirely on you.'

'Have it your own way. You haven't grown any.'

'Should I? I'm twenty.'

'I know.'

Felicity began to look a little anxiously from one to the other. 'She did very well in her finals!' she finally announced.

'The results aren't out yet, Flick!' Genny murmured repressively.

'No matter, you'll manage all right!' Ingo returned dryly, his sparkling eyes taunting her. 'Of all God's creatures, the most beautiful and the thinnest-skinned just has to be a woman.'

'Then you're not blind, darling!' Felicity said with her smiling rosy mouth.

'Listen to her!' Ingo jeered. 'Endowed to a fantastic degree. You look great, Flick, as always.'

Don't mind me, Genny thought, trying to look indifferent. Pray keep your insults for Flick's daughter. As it was she was giving out radiations that were fairly detectable to Ingo's perfect sight. His glance lingered on her speculatively before he turned back to Felicity.

'If you like to climb in, I'll have a word with them inside and collect your luggage. I have to be back on Tandarro by three o'clock. An American buyer is flying in, Dan Howell. You don't know him. He'll be staying over for a few days, I imagine.'

'Just a solitary male?' asked Felicity.

'Yes.' Ingo tapped his cousin's cheek. 'And kindly don't go getting involved with him. Did you say something, Giannina?'

'No.'

'No sound is still the same. You can tell me what you were thinking later. I hear you've got a boy-friend.'

'That's natural, isn't it?'

'I suppose it is, doe-eyes! You'll probably have a score of them, all with different names.'

'I can't wait.'

'A sad fate. Wouldn't it be better to settle for one man?'

'Maybe I already have,' Genny said, raising her eyes to him for a second only.

'It helps if you know it,' he replied.

'What is all this leading to, children?' Felicity inquired. 'Not another one of your fearful battles?'

'No, of course not. Ingo likes playing the tough guy, don't you, Ingo?'

'Sure, cherub!'

'You haven't called me that in a long time.'

'It describes you—sometimes—if you miss those smouldering almond eyes. Go along with Flick like a good girl. I'll shower you with attention once we get home.'

Felicity started off gaily and Genny went to follow her, stayed by Ingo's detaining hand. 'That was a pretty exuberant welcome. I've missed you.'

'And to think I was worrying about coming!' she said with piquant malice.

'That's it, Genny, hurl yourself into the attack.'

'I might even hurt you,' she gibed.

'No way, baby, tempting as it is to you. After such a long absence you might at least deign to look at me.'

'I'm too smart for that! I might get accidentally hypnotised.'

'Try it.'

'I'm game enough.'

'I don't think there can be any doubt about that. Whoever thought of mixing eyes that get darker and darker with silver shaded hair?' he asked whimsically.

'The same mysterious Being who put silver chips in

your face. Brilliant, and an unfair advantage because they see too much.'

Ingo tilted her chin and held it, his thumb pressing lightly against the tiny cleft. 'One big happy family again, Giannina?'

'Don't call me that!'

'Why not, it's your name. It even suits you. You're an exotic little mixture. Of course, if you prefer Brat we'll settle for that. Your hair still curls the way it used to when you were five years old.'

'Fantastic as it may seem to you, it just grows that way!' she snapped.

'Gossamer.' He took a strand and pulled it rather painfully.

'I'm not looking for trouble,' she hissed at him, leaning forward a little.

'Why, Giannina, it follows you around. Didn't you know? Flick's just a pussycat beside you.'

She jerked her head away from him, giving a funny little muffled exclamation. 'Maybe it's best to let you run on ... and on ... any kind of chit-chat from me only maddens you.'

'No, it's intoxicating!' He laughed under his breath. 'However, if you don't smile at me I just might shove you out of the plane.'

'I thought you scorned a woman's smiles.'

'Not yours. Remember I knew you when you were cutting your baby teeth. It's a shock to me the way you behave now.'

Genny tossed her head. 'Maybe I'll think of something to make up for it.'

'I've thought of the very thing now. Want to hear?'

'No, thank you, Ingo!' she said coolly.

'Well, I've done my best. It's plain you're still bent on being the uncivilised child.'

'That's funny!'

'*Very!*' The sun was strong on his dark, handsome face. 'You might dread it, but this visit you're going to face yourself.'

'Not to mention you.'

'It might be the same thing.'

She flung out her hand in confusion and he caught it. 'Now what?'

'The minute you set eyes on me you try to turn me into a puppet,' she hurled at him.

'*Giannina!*' He only smiled at her, a swift flash of light across his face, and she hesitated.

'Flick's looking this way. Don't let's argue for her sake.'

'Right! It's not important now anyway. There's plenty of time. Get in the plane. In many ways Flick raised a bright child, but then again she hasn't taught you a thing about all that twittering women do. You I have to gag.'

'Twittering drives you mad. Don't deny it, Ingo, I know you.'

'Still it's restful sometimes!' His shining eyes were studying her with attention.

'Sally twitters, doesn't she?' Genny burst out.

'Now that you mention it, she does burble a lot of meaningless things.'

'You're a cruel devil!'

'Dear me!' he teased.

'I mean it!'

'Why?'

'Sally's in love with you. It would be simplicity itself to put her out of her misery.'

'As opposed to what?' inquired Ingo.

'Marrying her. It happens, I hear. Remember Tandarro needs an heir.'

'I'm going to be around a long time, Giannina.'

'Yes, but you want a son, don't you?'

35

'Sure I do. I even want the right woman.'

'I don't believe it!' Genny challenged him, her eyes enormous.

'For breeding purposes, that is!'

'Oh!' she said in a maddened, impatient manner. 'Every time I see you I want to kick you in the shins.'

'You can't afford to, you rash little cat.'

'I have a feeling I'm going to try pretty soon!'

'Remember the last time!' he warned her, not in the least playfully.

'I remember. Some people think you're a hero, an Outback king, but they're not aware of the other side of you.'

'At least *you* are. Now that you've suggested it, I'll give some thought to marrying Sally. I can well believe she'll make an excellent mother.'

'Yes, you don't really need a *wife*!'

'Now why is that so painful to you?'

Genny tried to pull away. 'Oh, go to the devil, Ingo.'

'Little worry on that score, I imagine you'll join me. What about this admirer, lover of yours, which?'

'He's actually just a friend, as you very well know. Anyway, I've invited him out.'

'Oh my, and me with my jealous streak.'

'What a joke!' she shot back.

'Who are you to say if I get jealous or not? I really care about you. When you grow out of the awkward, undisciplined schoolgirl stage, I'm going to treat you quite differently altogether.'

'I'm grown up now, and you know it.'

'I mean *properly*,' he insisted.

'No reprieve, I see.'

'No, the war's still on. I could, of course, knock over all the barriers, but I want you to kick them over yourself. Do you cry in your sleep?' he asked suddenly.

'Never about you!'

36

'I wish I could make sure of that, but enough of this idle chatter. Poor old Flick is making inscrutable signs through the window.'

'Probably she can't think of anything else to do. Come on, Ingo, let's fly away.'

'That's my girl, and it had better be soon.' His arm shot out abruptly, half turning her towards the light aircraft. Some faint violence in his face filled Genny with fright and confusion. Will I ever learn? she thought plaintively as she trudged towards the plane. Felicity's questioning eyes were upon her, so she threw up her head trying for a bright smile. The vivid, beautiful blue sky arched overhead, cloudless, in bright contrast to the blood-red soil. She was trembling right through with uncertainty. She climbed into the plane and took a seat behind her mother, unexpectedly subdued, her dark eyes lowered.

'What was that all about?' Felicity asked. 'You were quite a length of time.'

'You know how it is. Ingo had a few things to tell me. He's delighted to see you looking so well.'

'Go on. Dear Ingo!' Felicity said, and stretched very gracefully. 'I wonder what this Howell man will be like?'

'Is it important?' asked Genny.

'Don't be dim-witted, darling. Pleasant company is always an asset. I imagine if he's buying Tandarro stock he has money.'

'There's money everywhere out here. Why not reach out and grab it?'

Felicity brightened. 'That's great, darling. I was afraid you'd want me to settle into a dreary widowhood.'

'You'd never be happy that way,' said Genny, and her mother sighed happily.

'Ingo looks sweeter than ever. Madly, impossibly handsome.'

'Ingo *sweet*?' Genny interjected. 'I could find maybe ten thousand words to describe him, but sweet wouldn't be one of them.'

'He's sweet to me.'

'That's your special magic. You don't arouse the beast in him.'

'I have no motive for wanting to. I just live for the day when things come right again between you two. You could have smiled at him, darling. Why the poker face?'

'It's the only way I know to control myself. Here comes the great man, anyway.' Genny turned her head and her eyes fastened on his compulsively. He looked up and caught her, his thick black hair with a crisp wave in it showing no trace of brown in the dazzling sunlight. She freed her eyes with an exaggerated little toss of her head, grateful for the fact that Felicity had slipped into the co-pilot's seat.

A few minutes more and Ingo had joined them, his winged black eyebrows drawn together in concentration, turning the aircraft into the path of the sun. Genny fastened her seat belt and sat back, never really at ease until the moment when she knew they were airborne. After that it was Felicity's job to supply all the answers to Ingo's questions and fill him in with the city gossip, which oddly enough he appeared to listen to and laugh at. Something in Felicity's make-up made her at ease in any man's company, which in turn most men found relaxing, their pleasure increased by her enchanting appearance. Genny gazed steadily at the clouds beneath her, feeling lonely. She wouldn't have interrupted her mother for the world, but Felicity was giving Ingo entirely the wrong impression about a lot of things, notably Genny's affairs. Flick's heady, honey-tongued chatter had drawn a few acerbic comments, but for the most part Ingo looked amused, the expression of his darkly bronze face indulgent. Genny turned her head languidly along the seat. She was never a great traveller. Twenty minutes later, Ingo's voice broke through her consciousness.

'Give us a chance, Genny. Aren't you going to contribute anything to the conversation, or have you just come along to catch up on your sleep?'

'No, for the endless pleasure of your company!' she said sweetly, brushing her eyes.

'At least your heart's in the right place.'

'Genny is just about the perfect daughter!' Felicity said proudly.

'Hear that, Giannina?'

Genny ignored the mockery. 'Thanks, Flick!'

'I think your education needs broadening and I'll say it out loud,' Ingo asserted.

'That should be easy out here, Ingo *dear*!'

'There wasn't anywhere else to go, was there, Giannina?'

'Weren't you listening to Flick? She said Bali.'

'You'd run right into the Wet.'

'I could do that here!' she protested.

'Much less likely, though we've had a run of good seasons!'

'When is Trish coming?' Felicity asked, trying to divert them.

'The perfect sidetrack! Some time next week, Flick!' he answered with his cool arrogance.

Genny's eyes fixed themselves broodingly on a point somewhere between his wide shoulders. 'Why don't you ever ask your mother out?'

He swung his head back to her his eyes like a lightning flash in his imperious dark face. 'Did you rehearse that?'

39

'No, it just came out. You're a ruthless person, aren't you, Black Ingo?'

'Yes, brutal, and you're not safe from me, though you pick your moments.'

Felicity's blue eyes were appealing. 'Genny, Genny, what's got into you? Where are your manners?'

'It's all right, Flick,' Ingo said, 'I like cantankerous little females. I just want to pick them up like spitting kittens and watch them rage.'

'It just so happens, Ingo, that I was serious. If your mother's as beautiful as everyone says she is ...'

'Leave it!' His voice had the cut of a whiplash.

She flashed him one emotion-laden look, holding up her hands. 'All right, all right! No mistaking that warning. I wouldn't dream of upsetting the mighty cattle baron.'

'Actually, darling, you're embarrassing your mother!' Felicity pointed out mildly.

Genny shrugged. 'Then excuse me while I doze off. It doesn't matter a damn if I'm here or not anyway. You and Ingo are the adults.'

Unexpectedly Felicity went off into peals of laughter. 'Baby girl, don't be silly!'

'That's what she is, just what she sounds, a tragic child. She needs lots of reassuring,' Ingo said mockingly.

'I'm woman enough to hate you, Ingo darling.'

'Hate me, what next? If one could take the slightest notice of you.'

'She doesn't hate you at all, Ingo,' Felicity said consolingly, 'though sometimes I think this kind of thing will go on and on for ever.'

'You mean Giannina nurses it along a lot. A good beating mightn't go astray.'

'And wouldn't you like to do it?' Genny muttered rebelliously, but very quietly.

'Yes, and I heard that. Trouble is I wouldn't know when to stop.'

'Well, I guess a man's bound to be feudal out here.'

'Why make it sound an unforgivable crime?'

'Because it is!' she said heatedly. 'I'm not thrilled by dictators.'

'Tut, tut!' he teased.

'Not another word, I beg of you.' Felicity turned back to Genny, wagging her finger.

Genny's cheeks burned. 'Why make it sound *my* speciality, Flick? Ingo's just as much to blame.'

'But we're flying over *my* territory, little one. My world. You're giving a whole lot of cheek to a tyrant on his home ground. That doesn't strike me as smart.'

'Are we really over Tandarro?' Felicity cried. 'Let me look.'

'You can't yet, Flick. You'll have to wait until we descend. We're actually on the border of the desert, coming in to Tandarro right now.'

Sudden excitement flared in Felicity's pink-and-white skin. 'Oh, golly, what does it feel like to be rich and powerful?'

'Delightful.'

'No one should be too rich when there's so much real poverty in the world,' Genny said severely.

'Shut up, Gen!' he said lazily. 'Don't bite the hand that feeds you.'

'It's exactly what you *don't* do!'

'What does she mean, Flick?' Ingo turned to his cousin.

'I don't know, dear. She's very spirited, we have to take that into account.'

'I know she'd like to sink her white little teeth into me,' he agreed lazily.

'I thought she meant she was going on a hunger strike.'

41

'I need a lot of patience with you two!' Genny said, and suddenly laughed.

'Keep it up, baby, that sounds beautiful.'

'Thanks, Ingo. I reserve my best laughs for you.'

'You'll find I've got something lined up for you!'

'Oh, really, what?' She leaned forward, tilting her head so that she could look into his face. Almost certainly she expected him to smile at her or say something sarcastic, but he just stared into her eyes, so disquietingly that she moved nervously. 'What, Ingo?' she almost whispered, her beautiful mouth parted, her dark eyes startled. If she had been standing, she was sure she would have been swaying.

'Something too good for you in every way, you little brat!'

He turned away from her, but she continued to scrutinise his dark profile. 'I didn't really need persuading to come out here. I really love it,' she confessed.

'Oh yes?'

'You *know* I do.'

'Do you take your moods in turns?' he inquired.

'I don't know what you mean.'

'You sound remarkably sweet and submissive now.'

'Yes, you do!' Felicity confirmed. 'You should hear her with Dave!'

'Is he for real?' Ingo asked.

'He *loves* me!' Genny burst out, when it was the last thing in the world she intended to say.

'Then he's ninety-nine per cent crazy!'

'It depends on how you see me.'

'Yes,' said Felicity, totally fair, 'it's pathetic the way all the boys fall in love with her and she brushes them all off.'

'*The boys fall in love with her*,' Ingo muttered with savage amusement. 'Don't be such a damn fool, Flick.'

42

'It isn't at all strange, darling. Genny is a beautiful girl.'

'And tremendously unready for love and marriage, for example.'

'So are *you*!' Genny fired at him, her heart thudding.

'Perhaps we're scarred, baby. Both of us.'

'Ingo?' Felicity asked uncertainly, bewildered by the distinctly sombre note in his voice. 'Are you blaming me for something I've done to Genny?'

'Your catastrophic marriages?'

'Leave Flick alone,' Genny said in some anger, reaching over and gripping his shoulder.

He lifted his own hand and caught her fingers tightly. 'You might find yourself over my knee.'

'You're hurting me, Ingo.'

'Forgive me, *please!*' He pulled at her hand and carried it to his mouth.

Such an exquisite dart of pain shot through her that she almost moaned. 'Let me go!'

'You really are crazy, you know that?' demanded Felicity.

Genny drew her hand back quickly. It was trembling. 'It's all right, Flick, he's winning now, but just wait for the next thrilling episode!'

'You scare me, you two,' her mother pouted.

'Don't take any notice, Flick!' Ingo said with his beautiful, rare smile. 'Your tranquillity is irresistible after Genny's demented behaviour. I like the new hairstyle, it's ravishing. The ultimate in witchcraft!'

Genny groaned, but Felicity flushed with pleasure. 'You didn't prefer it that bit longer?'

'No. You look younger than ever. You even make *me* feel old!'

'You? Why, you're impossibly dynamic!' Felicity cried.

43

'Don't mind me!' Genny interjected. 'You're both sending me witless.'

'Then put your silver head back and ignore us,' Ingo suggested dryly. 'If you're not eager for a few compliments, I am. No use to look for them from you!'

'I think you've very handsome, Ingo, but I don't think we'll ever meet the woman who makes you surrender.'

'Surrender?' he crowed, consumed with his own male superiority.

'Yes, beaten to your knees, struck by one of little old Cupid's darts.'

'God!' he said, his mouth amused.

'I'd be happy to see it happen!' Genny said softly.

'I can barely wait myself.'

'I bet Sally's wangled herself an invitation!' Felicity said, following a logical line of thought.

'She's been throwing out some pretty heavy hints,' agreed Ingo.

'Why don't you marry the girl?' Felicity asked.

'Have a heart, Flick!'

'Remember you're *king*!' Genny threw in with intensity.

'An enormous responsibility, I assure you.'

'It certainly requires some monstrous acts!' she said tartly.

Unexpectedly he laughed, and Ingo smiling or laughing was irresistible, his sparkling eyes dancing, his hard, handsome mouth unbelievably softened. The fragments of magic. All the old memories returned. Ingo teaching her how to swim and to dive, how to ride and cut cattle. Ingo making her a wreath of wildflowers to wear in her hair. Ingo showing her the cave drawings and explaining all the old myths and legends. Ingo pointing out the Sky Country. *That* Ingo she loved.

44

There! she'd said it, the forbidden word. Ingo had no place in his life for love or any of the softer sentiments. Ingo was the man in command, freed from the slavery of women. Only one had ever really hurt him, his own mother. The beloved woman, the woman who bore him. No other would ever get the opportunity.

As if completely tuned in to her thoughts, Ingo swung his head abruptly. 'Damn it, you've got tears in your eyes!'

'I haven't!' she said, blinking fiercely.

'You have, you little fool!'

'Children, children!' said Felicity helplessly.

'Surely a few tears don't bother you?' demanded Genny.

'Yours do!'

'Yes, they make you angry. I was crying for you, Ingo, if you must know.'

'I can't imagine why!' Felicity turned around quickly, searching her daughter's face with concern. 'Darling girl, what's the matter?'

'Not a darn thing!'

'Maybe it's her first love affair. They tell me they're unsettling!' Ingo said tersely.

'What do you think?' Genny asked deliberately. 'Or haven't you had one?'

'I'm a coward,' he answered tersely.

'Maybe you are. You won't let anyone get near you.'

'I'll tell you, Giannina, *you* get right under my skin!'

'This is all very strange!' said Felicity, appalled and fascinated by these exchanges, clashing with deadly intent.

Ingo glanced at her, seeing the faint distress in her sky-blue eyes. 'Felicity, the tender, the gentle, how did you ever come to have such a blazing little hellcat for a daughter?'

45

'I can't accept that she's anything like that. Only with *you*.'

'Oh, so I've got to take all the credit?'

Felicity smiled. 'It would seem so, darling. Fantastic, I know!'

'*We* sure lost our way somehow!' Genny said derisively. 'It's you who's vanished completely. I'm still the same.'

'Would you mind repeating that, please?' Ingo held up his hand. 'I find it almost impossible to believe!'

'I said I'm still the same. I've just lost my companion and dearest friend.'

'Don't you think it's because you're beautiful and a woman?'

Genny grimaced. 'Ah, now I see it quite clearly. Woman. Miss out all the rest!'

'*Mystery!*' Ingo said, and laughed a little. 'I still love you, baby, whether you believe it or not.'

'Now that's unusual in a man, fidelity,' Felicity said, apparently quite sincerely, not only rejecting but chasing away all thought of her own misadventures.

'Deviations aren't only reserved for men, Flick,' Ingo pointed out, rather kindly for him when he had no patience with Felicity's breathless involvements, and worse still, held her responsible for Genny's multiple anxieties and the tensions she had endured with precisely such a mother. Felicity was very loving and demonstrative with her daughter, but all things were relevant. Felicity simply wasn't capable of her daughter's depth of feeling, nor did she have Genny's intelligence or extreme sensitivity. Nevertheless he smiled at her and Felicity purred with satisfaction. The conversation went on, peaceably this time, for Genny disturbed them no more.

Although Felicity never said anything of any great importance and avoided controversial matters like the plague, she had an extensive circle of friends, even women friends, and men of all ages were kindly disposed towards her, Ingo included. Maybe it should teach me something! Genny thought wryly. Painful as it was to accept, men really didn't like confident or overly intelligent women. They could deny it all they liked and write long favourable articles about liberty and equality, but in their hearts they never meant a word of it. Such articles sold, but they were hypocrisy nonetheless. Nothing had changed since life in the caves.

Ingo, at any rate, would have been at home there. Challenging the elements, wild marauding beasts, assembling a community with himself for the leader, hauling a woman off by her hair. Ingo was violent. He was also the most elegant, civilised man in the world, but that was only a veneer, a thick coat of polish. There was some element in Ingo, Genny feared. He disturbed her enormously and worst of all, he charmed her too frequently, the sight and the sound of him. She could still feel the tingle of his mouth on her skin.

She made a small helpless sound, appropriate even in a caveman's mate, and settled more comfortably into her seat. Soon they would touch down at Tandarro, the capital of Ingo's world. She had only herself to blame for moving into his arena, the most dangerous and the most beautiful place in the world.

CHAPTER THREE

DAN HOWELL had never been so enchanted in his life. Not one but two beautiful blondes, hanging on his every word. Except that he was fifty and admirably in control of himself, it would have gone to his head. A Texan, and very proud of it, he looked not unlike the hero's kinsman in every Western Genny had ever seen, with a ruddy, sun-scarred face, a powerful broad-shouldered frame just starting to get heavy, his thick hair bleached to flax and his light blue eyes, used to looking through vast distances, creased and piercing, but very friendly. Both women took to him at once, and even Aunt Evelyn looked mildly intrigued, all three showing considerable unfeigned interest in his part of the world and the Texan way of life.

Given such interest and attention Dan waxed lyrical, in his pleasant drawl, not going on about Texas' tremendous size in the face of the State of Queensland's immensity and the cattle empire he was on, but providing them all with stirring examples of wealth acquired, adventure and enterprise, the enormous drive that had opened up the American West at pretty much the same time as Queensland was being settled. Listening to Dan, who had known hardship as well as the rewards of building up a fine, progressive ranch, they could almost see everything he talked about happening before their very eyes. Dan was a born raconteur with a singular dry wit and Ingo, his host, encouraged him with his anecdotes with no thought of Howell, the buyer, but because he liked the man and was enjoying his company.

'My goodness, I can see it all so clearly!' Felicity said, her lovely countenance transfixed.

'Thank you, ma'am!'

'So you really say that?' she asked, enchanted.

'We do. I don't know when I've ever seen a prettier woman either.'

Pink covered Felicity's cheeks like a gauzy veil. 'Now, Dan, I'm immunised against flattery.'

'The simple truth,' he assured her.

Pleasure raced through Felicity's veins like champagne. 'I don't know that you've mentioned Mrs Howell?'

Dan shook his flaxen head. 'No deliberate omission. There is no Mrs Howell, but sooner or later it has to come to me.'

'I don't believe it, Dan, you're a bachelor.'

'Fairly caught tonight!'

Evelyn just prevented herself from snorting and Genny caught Ingo's eye. He looked perversely entertained, marvellously attractive with his mocking smile as he stared right back into Genny's face.

'Why don't I show you the night sky?' suggested Felicity, who had found through tried and true experience that the simplest approach was best.

'Do you mean all of us?' Ingo inquired sardonically.

'You've seen it before. Dan may not be used to our celestial displays.'

'True. I've never had the Southern Cross pointed out to me.' Dan smiled, a little disconcerted by the faint tension he surprised in Genny's face. Because she was a youngster he didn't dare look at her, but he found her fascinating, with her silver-gilt curls rioting around her piquant face, her eyes so dark and velvety one could luxuriate in them. She was very beautiful with her intoxicating youth and her distinctly Italianate look, but her face wasn't joyful. It was passionate, fiery, the mou full, the chin faintly cleft, but it wasn't a happy fa Some soft kind of desolation was there for all her sl ravishing smile. A broken heart, perhaps. Young took things so much to heart, especially one who lo like that. But why should she be looking at the inn stranger in their midst with such controlled app sion? Dan smiled at her, trying to reassure he didn't know what, and she smiled back at him taking his breath away.

Ingo, aware of Genny's habitual anxieties and the reason for them, intercepted Dan's eyes seeing the fascination in his face. 'All right, Dan, I can well see such an experience might be hard to come by another time. Flick, I might tell you, is an inveterate Circe.'

'There you are, Dan, be warned!' Felicity said gaily.

'Heaven help me, there's nothing I want to do more. One of these days I might even be able to show you our Texan sky. It's pretty big. You've seen it, Ingo, tell her!'

Ingo grinned. 'Honestly, I don't know which is the more beautiful.'

'You're only saying that so you won't get into an argument,' bridled Felicity.

'Anyway, Flick, you're talking to a man of consequence. Dan has a great property!'

'Well, maybe not the size of yours. Even I can't get used to these immense holdings you have over here. The ranch house couldn't compare with this palace, that's for sure. It seems pretty remarkable set down in the wilds. I can never quite follow why there are so many English mansions in the Australian outback.'

'Dreams of home,' Ingo said, finishing off his drink. 'The deep-rooted desire to recreate the ancestral home in the wild bush. Everyone knows the British are accentric; nothing spared to impose order and good taste in the most unlikely places. As far as I know we haven't neglected that side of it!'

'It's quite a place!' Dan said truthfully, not altogether at home with the Faulkner eccentricities, the great chandeliers and the heirloom silver, the antique furniture and the paintings, with a whole row of old family portraits down through the years, formidable-looking men and overruled-looking women looking out rather austerely from their gilded frames. On the other

50

hand, Dan decided there and then, he would make an attempt to redecorate the ranch house when he got back home. Maybe get the right people in to do it. He certainly had the money. He might as well sink it into some very high-class furnishings and paintings and things. Women usually took care of that side of it, but in fact Tandarro had been designed, built and furnished from top to bottom by George Douglass-Faulkner, an English 'gentleman selector' reminiscent of the style of the splendid two storied mansion he had been born in and which had been inherited by Edward, his eldest brother. His desire to make his own way and build up his own dynasty had led him to Australia, through New South Wales into Queensland, where there was intense competition to take up large leases on magnificent grazing land. Originally intending to invest in sheep, Faulkner turned his attention to cattle, becoming so prosperous after a number of years that he was able to bring out his two younger brothers and their families.

Dan privately considered the lofty proportions of the dining room with its solid, dark-hued opulence and heavy Victorian furniture as too 'old world', too rich and massive for his taste, but he had to admit Faulkner looked as at home at the head of the long gleaming table as he did in the saddle. Dan was an ardent admirer of the younger man as a cattleman and breeder; close to, in his own home, Ingo Faulkner seemed very much Dan's idea of the English aristocrat worked into a more easy-going shape in the country of his adoption. There were men in plenty who lived like kings in Texas and it was certainly true on Tandarro, a property so big that it was more like a self-contained kingdom with Faulkner, the benevolent but all-powerful ruler. Miss Evelyn, the elderly aunt, though still handsome, was the sort of woman Dan avoided at all times, but Felicity and her daughter Genny were perfect, as deli-

51

cate and feminine and as carefully guarded as any other Faulkner possession.

The girl Genny, Faulkner called Giannina, with a wonderful balance between indulgence and a dreadful teasing. One had a way of speaking and the other interjecting that Dan found curious. He couldn't quite follow either of them, and there was an unnameable something in Faulkner's striking face every time he looked at his young cousin. Such a beautiful and intelligent girl Dan would have cherished, yet Faulkner seemed oblivious to her fine-drawn look, sending any number of flippant little darts to her which she instantly returned. It wasn't Dan's way. He liked to put a woman way up there on a pedestal, far from this intriguing challenging that was going on. Felicity too, he sensed, was puzzled by the coolly tempestuous thrust and parry. It wasn't her way either.

When they had gone, taking the jeep because there was a splendid vantage point from Spirit Hill, the scene of live magic and ritual sacred dances, there was silence at the table where they still lingered over coffee. Aunt Evelyn, resplendent in an ageless mauve gown that had cost an enormous amount when she bought it many years before, thought it best to express her dignified disapproval.

'For all I care we may never see them again, but I beg of you, Genny, don't upset yourself unnecessarily.'

'You know Flick! She was just flattered, and he seems a very nice man.'

'The life you've led often makes me cry.'

'Evvy, don't excite yourself!' Ingo said carelessly.

'I can't help it. The way Felicity was acting reminds me of the last time.'

'Not Hughie, surely?'

'No, not Hughie, the other one, what was his name?'

'Stewart,' Genny said obediently.

'It's humiliating! The man comes to buy stock and Felicity runs away with him.'

'Please, Aunt Evelyn, I love my mother best in the world. She's like a child. She doesn't realise that she fills us all with apprehension. I'm sure this is only a pleasant diversion.'

'We'll give them an hour, then we'll go and look for them!' Ingo said, half flippantly, half intentionally. 'I'd say Dan's voted Flick the prettiest woman he's ever laid eyes on, but you, my repressed little Giannina, knocked him rotten.'

'I beg your pardon?' Genny turned her aureoled head, the light shining on the flicked-up curls.

'No news, Giannina, you know when a man's looking at you, you just feel you have to hide it.'

'Except that I didn't notice,' she retorted.

'I did,' Aunt Evelyn said, somewhat severely. 'It's a good thing you're just a child.'

'No, Ev, there's been a big change over the years. Not a lot of progress in other ways ...'

'If it's all right with you, Aunt Evelyn, I'm going to escape for a little,' Genny said hurriedly. 'I hope you like the records I brought you.'

'My dearest child, thank you once again. It's so good of you to think of me—and the books, all my favourite authors.'

'Remember her when you make your will!' said Ingo, his brilliant eyes on Genny's tinted face, the wild apricot that stained her high cheekbones.

'As you very well know I've already made it, not that Father left me a great deal,' replied Aunt Evelyn.

'I should have thought you were a rich woman!' Ingo said, and laughed at her.

'I'll tell you now that I've divided it equally. One part to you, my beloved nephew, and the other to Giannina, who I fear will need it with such a mother.'

Ingo shook his head, his dark face sparkling with humour. 'Evvy, I'm proud of you. I promise you I'll spend it all wisely. As for Giannina, who seems to be struck speechless for once, she should fall on her knees and thank you. With all that money she won't even have to marry.'

Aunt Evelyn threw up her hands. 'I couldn't bear it if she were to become an old maid. Look at me! Father always told me there wasn't a man worthy of me.'

'Couldn't you have decided for yourself?'

'Oh, I wish I had now. I might have had children of my own. However, as you know, I love both of you, notwithstanding the fact that you argue all the time.'

'It seems to me being an unmarried lady is no disgrace!' Genny said very earnestly. 'Surely it's better than being an unhappy wife?'

'I dare say!' Aunt Evelyn said quietly. 'It's just that I've never had ...'

'I know, I know.' The tender-hearted Genny leapt up from the table and came round to fling her arms about Aunt Evelyn's thin, square shoulders, her beautiful dark eyes with tears in them.

'Girls, girls, we can't go on like this!' Ingo shoved back his chair and stood up. 'I can scarcely prevent myself from breaking down. Come on, Evvy, you may be torn about being an old maid, but don't forget you reared me. That's something.'

'Yes, and I'm proud of you. I know how kind and good you really are,' his aunt said quietly.

'You'll have to tell me about it some time,' Genny flashed out irrepressibly, 'I can't see it myself.'

Aunt Evelyn patted her hand, forcing a smile. 'I think you can. My father was a man of rigid and old-fashioned ideas about women: a remarkable man, a strong man, but Ingo has something neither my father nor his own father had.'

'Don't tell her, Evvy, let her find out for herself.'

'That might be the best thing. Now if you two will excuse me, I'll start on one of the new books Genny brought me. I'm quite a fan of Mary Stewart's, especially those old thriller-romances.'

'Very proper in a woman. Where would we be without romance?' Ingo held his aunt's chair, bending to brush his mouth against her firm, unlined cheek. 'Don't worry about Flick. She always falls on her feet.'

'It's not Felicity so much I worry about, it's this child here.'

'I'll worry about her,' Ingo assured her.

'I know you do.' Aunt Evelyn withdrew smilingly, her back straight, her silver-streaked black head held high.

Genny watched her, feeling singularly upset. 'Poor old Evvy!' she said softly.

Ingo shook his head. 'I'm afraid I can't feel sorry for Miss Evelyn Faulkner of Tandarro. On the other hand, I might have felt sorry for her husband.'

'What a rotten thing to say!'

'Darling, Evvy's becoming more and more mellow. She was quite a tartar in her younger days and incurably haughty.'

'How else would she be, the way she was brought up?'

'We all suffer one way or the other. Look at you.'

'Yes, look at me,' Genny echoed ironically.

'I have been all evening, more or less.'

'You've taken great care to hide your glances from me.'

'Naturally! I enjoy that little patrician air of yours. It sits oddly with your passionate mouth.'

'Don't talk such rubbish!' she snapped.

'Hasn't Dave told you?'

'On the contrary, it's never entered the conversation.'

'Now you're making me really anxious. Tell me a bit more about his extraordinary behaviour.'

His attitude was careless, his lean body faultlessly arranged, one hand pushing against the table, the other shifting a crystal wineglass, yet his voice had an imperative note to it. It really got to her, her sadness transmuted to a sweet irritability.

'You're damned well not going to ruin any of my romances!'

'*Your* romances!' he scoffed at her, reaching out suddenly and drawing her towards him.

She swallowed dryly, feeling sizzled at his touch. His vivid dark face was openly mocking her, her own face was vaguely alarmed. Obeying a totally uncontrollable instinct, she began to rain small blows at him with her free hand so that he had to spin her like a doll, locking her virtually a prisoner within the hard circle of his arms. Her slight body lolled forward like a flower, her back to him, fighting the strength of his linked hands, the beginnings of a wild hysteria in her. She had to concentrate furiously on beating him off. It was unbearable to be so close to him.

'Stop it!' She dug her nails into him and he held her harder.

'If you want me to treat you gently, Genny, this isn't the way to go about it!'

'You're so ... so ...'

'Go on.'

'Let me go, Ingo!' she said, her breathing deep and urgent. She twisted her head back and looked into his eyes. Their silver glitter shocked her, the turbulent vitality, even menace. She could feel herself go white. 'Please, Ingo!' she whispered. the will to defy him dying. The wild resistance of a moment ago was shattered. She hadn't a hope against such dark, frightening energy, a man's physical strength. Tension and a hard

56

recklessness were there in his face, danger and excitement flashing around them like tongues of light. A soft shiver ran through her and she turned in his arms, her body playing tricks on her as it came to rest against him, curving trustingly like a child.

He made a sound of complete and utter exasperation, holding her more gently now almost without his volition, though the tremor was still in her body. 'What are you frightened of?' he asked tautly. 'Even your lashes are wet.'

She turned her head along his hard chest, her voice muffled. 'I don't *mean* to do the things I do. Did I scratch you? I'm sorry.'

'Oh, please don't try to comfort me,' he said acidly. 'I'm Black Ingo, remember.'

'But I love you!' she said passionately. 'At least I used to love you, only something's happened between us. Show me your hand.'

'Oh, go to the devil!' he said, hard and relentless.

'You throw me off balance,' she persisted. 'You keep teasing me. How much do you think I can take?'

'*You* can take! God. Let's reflect on that. How long has it been this time? Six or seven hours, and I'm ready to strangle you.'

'But you're so appallingly cruel to me.'

'You pitchforked into *me*, might I remind you.'

'So I did,' she agreed. 'I can't for the life of me see why you want me here.'

'I'm none too certain myself.'

She drew a breath like a tortured child, letting him cradle her as though it were vital she rely on his strength, filled with an intense desire to keep him as he was at this minute, unwillingly tender, the thud of his heart striking into her. For no reason at all, on rare occasions, their antagonisms became invisible. She felt undeniably and utterly safe and needed. Precisely a

57

possession, but someone, in an unguarded moment, special.

'What is this?' he said beneath his breath, bending his head so that the tips of her curls tickled his chin. 'Some kind of reward?'

'You usedn't to mind!' she appealed.

'I can't believe that now. You simply didn't have this intolerably slender body. What would Dave think if he could see you now?'

'What do you mean?' She lifted her head, her dark eyes bewildered.

His white teeth actually snapped, his eyes losing what little serenity they had attained. 'Excuse me, Giannina,' he said, putting her forcibly away from him. 'We'll pick up this conversation at another time, perhaps in a year or so. It's too beautiful a night to stay indoors. Do you want to come for a ride?'

'A ride?' she echoed.

'Damn it, isn't that what I said? You'll have to get out of that expensive bit of nothing. We'll take the horses.'

Her small face, that had looked rather mortally endangered, flared into expectant life. The swift lurch of pleasure that shot through her was reflected in her eyes, lingering inexplicably on all the splendid dark arrogance she thought she would resist until the day she died. 'What a marvellous idea!'

'The only one I can think of if I want to save my soul.'

'Where shall we go?' she asked.

'Don't worry, I won't drag you off into the lignum.'

She reached out and touched the scratch on his hand briefly. 'I'm sorry about that.'

'I'll get even, never mind. Get cracking, Genny, I'm full of merciless, wild longing. Head me off. You've no idea how fragile you look.'

58

'Oughtn't we wait here for Flick?'

Ingo frowned. 'Flick can take care of herself. I imagine, to her wonder, that she's found out Dan is a gentleman.'

'Wouldn't it be lovely if it were true!'

'It is. There are quite a few of us.'

'Oh, you beauty!' She suddenly took a full turn around the room like an enthusiastic ten-year-old, the skirt of her chiffon dress flying about her legs, its vivid poppy red dazzling her golden tan. 'Just give me five minutes!'

'I thought I'd given you a lifetime.'

'So you have! It's just that I've got to make a temporary break from your dominance. Understand?'

'No, I don't! It suits you sometimes, which you conveniently manage to forget about.'

'I'm sure it's only temporary, Ingo.'

'If it isn't, I'll clear up all your confusions in a matter of minutes.'

Genny's eager, balletic movements came to a full stop. She stood wistfully at a little distance from him, staring up into his face. 'No, I have to do it myself, even if I don't know why. Please put some disinfectant on that scratch. It looks ragged.'

'I promise I will in a couple of days. Right now I want to look at it and make *you* look at it. It hurts so much, I'm lucky I'm alive!'

'It could have been worse!' she said uncertainly.

'In every way,' he said. 'You'll never really know.'

'I'm sure I've plagued you with scratches before.'

'That was a while back. You were about fourteen at the time, just turning into a terrible urchin. Your future husband had better study for his Black Belt.'

She smiled, intensely conscious of the dancing lights in his eyes. 'You tell him the kind of family he's marrying into!'

'He knew long ago.'

He was watching her in complete absorption and she turned abruptly away from him instinctively fighting his magnetism. 'Flick!' she said urgently. 'I don't suppose we would go via Spirit Hill?'

'Oh, Giannina!' he said with sharp amusement. 'Grow up!'

'That sounded like a prayer,' she said, surprised.

'I've tried everything else I can think of. If you're not down at the stables in under ten minutes, I won't wait.'

'Yes, you will. I'm used to your threats.'

'And I'm used to your reversals, you're a capricious little wretch. File your claws while you're at it!'

'I'll bring some cream back!' she promised, almost flying to the door, a slight graceful figure against the massive cedar double doors.

'Yes,' he said dryly, 'it could be fatal to overlook one of your scratches!'

The night sky was beautiful, the vast purple-veiled black dome spangled with millions of diamonds, swirling in currents, thousands gauzy and indistinct, thousands more burning brightly; blazing over the sandhills, the fantastic network of water channels, the ironstone ranges, the Timeless Land, the ancient home of the oldest tribes on earth. The air was heavy with flower scent, boronia, wild lime, the unusual little lilies that grew in thick clusters in amongst the river reeds, and directly above them, with shattering brilliance, the guardian of the Great South Land, the Southern Cross, holding dominion over the night sky. Its particular stars formed the perfect outline that had been worshipped for thousands of years before recorded history. Jirrunjoonga, the Guiding Star. Jirrunjoonga, the jewelled home of the Sky People.

Genny's face was uplifted to its eternal splendour. Tandarro at all times had a rare magic for her, but night was bewitching, the sound of chanting around distant fires, the unearthly howling of the dingoes, the song of the wind. She couldn't quite understand it, but she felt exultant. In the morning she might be Genny Mora. Tonight she was Giannina with magic in her bloodstream. The colt, Caspian, could race like the wind and she revelled in its speed, the responsiveness that made it such a joy to ride.

If she rode far enough and high enough to the crest of the hill country she could bring down an uncatch-able star, a perfect, extravagant diamond daisy. The wind was whipping through her hair, delighting her with its purity and flavour. The years she had been windswept! The halcyon years of Tandarro! The im-mense glittering of the stars seemed to be hypnotising her, she wanted passionately to abandon herself to this fantastic world, the world she had known through all the years of her childhood.

Her clear voice rose above the wind. 'I'll race you into that pocket of trees.'

Whether Ingo understood her or not, he gave her the advantage, switching through a walk into a full gallop.

Genny reined in under the trees and turned the colt's head about. 'Ingo, where are you?'

It was strangely silent with the breeze whispering around her, her pulses throbbing with a primitive kind of excitement, a frantic rhythm of life. It wasn't pos-sible that he was still behind her. She knew exactly the way he could ride, not to mention the speed of Red Dust, the big chestnut stallion. Nevertheless she made a small movement of worry, swinging her head about repeatedly, her eyes trying to pierce the fresh, fragrant gloom. 'Ingo, where the devil are you? Obviously I've

61

won and you can't bear to be beaten!' Her clear young voice began to vibrate a little wildly, puzzled and inexplicably threatened by the dark. A ghostly green firefly flicked past her head and she made a swipe at it, almost spooking the colt. '*Ingo!*'

'Lost someone?' Suddenly he was beside her, on foot, pulling her out of the saddle, his hands biting into the soft skin at her waist. 'Don't delude yourself, kiddo, you can't beat me at anything.'

'I'm promising myself I will!'

'That's obvious. Let's go down to the water. It will be cool there.'

'After that mad flight I'm nearly in favour of a swim,' she said.

'I'm not game to go as far as that!' he said dryly. 'Much too disturbing.'

'All right then, but for heaven's sake, I spent years splashing you.'

'Nothing remains static,' he retorted. 'Even *my* self-control has its limits!'

'You were such a comfort and encouragement to me then,' she said in a slightly melancholy fashion.

'And you were a very sweet child, a regular little cherub. The violent change overcame you at about thirteen or fourteen, I can't be sure. You began to hate me then.'

'No!'

'Oh *yes*!' he said quietly.

She looked up at him, surprised. 'You sound as though it's troubled you, and nothing has troubled you before!'

'Little idiot!' he exclaimed.

The lagoon, shining and very deep, was now clearly visible. 'Oh, doesn't it look inviting!'

'For safety's sake, we'll just sit on the bank.'

The splendid sheet of water was a place of live magic

with a legend attached to it. Lofty river gums lined its banks, scented acacias, long sprays of the flowering bauhinias, cream and pink and deepest magenta, the air heady with the sweet musky perfume of the bell-shaped lilies that grew thickly in among the river reeds. The leaves rustled on the night wind, the branches of the trees heavy with nesting birds that in the pre-dawn made the wild bush resound with their full-throated symphonies. Silent though they were now, Genny could almost hear their timeless music, the shrieking of the great colonies of corellas, the whistling and the sweet chirruping, the cello tones, and the high frenzied choruses by the massed choirs.

Ingo settled his back against the trunk of a slender gum with yellow citrus-scented blossom, drawing Genny down beside him and turning her so that her head rested against his bent knees. Almost immediately he collected small pebbles in his hand, sending them in a series of skipping flourishes across the silvery-sheened waters.

'That's a very well-practised technique!' she said idly.

'The one thing I can't teach you—how to throw. Women have a frightful aim.'

'They still manage to get what they want,' she observed.

'Don't I know!'

'It's beautiful, this place!' Genny said fervently. 'A hallowed spot. Remember the bellbird that used to nest here?'

'It's gone further up the creek. Along with the pelicans.'

'I think I could remain a captive here for ever!' she said, looking up at the blossoming, beautiful stars. 'Listen to the water running over those stones. Music! The sound of the wind and the pull of the stars. I never

63

feel this free in the city. There's not this wonderful communion with Nature. I love the way those willows drape themselves into the pool. Isn't this the home of a water nymph?'

'The one that got turned into a White Ibis, so the legend goes. Some nights she's visible, dancing over there on the far side.'

'Have you ever seen her?' she asked.

'No, I haven't, which is rather sad. I've seen all the wishing rings the boys leave about in the hope of a shadow dance.'

'That's interesting. I wonder how Flick's going?'

'Probably Dan's fallen under her influence. Woman magic beats all hell out of everything. Even the Sky People.'

'It's curious the way things don't touch her deeply. Poor old Hughie's only been dead a year.'

'Long enough! Surely you're not inviting my comments, Giannina? I've always had the strong impression you can't tolerate the slightness criticism of Flick.' Ingo sounded wry.

'I'm not criticising, I'm just remarking, and then only to you. You understand her, though I knew you never approve of these inevitable complications.' She gave a faint sigh, her small face shimmering like a pearl. 'It is strange, though, the way nothing has a deep effect on her.'

'When her actions have a far-reaching effect on *you*? Nothing can be done about Flick. She's very sweet and even lovable, but she's still a penance.'

'Don't say that!' she protested quickly.

'I don't have to convince you, Giannina, you know, so let's drop it. I was rather enjoying our unfamiliar harmony.'

'Yes, let's kiss and make up!' she said flippantly.

'What a good idea!'

She tensed. 'I was only fooling. We've never done anything like that.'

'What?'

'Oh, kiss and make up, you know. We're not the kissing kind.'

He bent his dark head, shadowing her face. 'That would be really funny if it were true.'

'Well, you know what I mean. I don't mean Sally or all those other sex objects, I mean us!'

'You're beginning to worry me. Flick may have done more damage than I thought.'

'Come to think of it, you do kiss Flick coming and going. Why not me?'

'Flick's easy to rain kisses on,' he said lightly.

'And I'm like Medusa with a head full of snakes!'

'Let's see!' He speared his hand into her silky curls, twisting her head back against his knee. 'No, the same gossamer soft strands. Suppose I start kissing you. Coming and going, that is.'

'Let's leave things the way they are now,' she said hastily.

'I *said* your education needs broadening. I carried it so far, I might as well take it the rest. Are you sure Dave's got red blood in his veins?'

'Sadist!'

'I don't like that. You really say the most unforgivable things.'

'And I don't like being the butt of your little jokes.'

'I'm not laughing and neither are you,' he said.

'I'm beginning to think I made a mistake in coming.'

'It's too late to do anything about it now!' Beneath the mocking humour was a hint of sensuality that filled her with an unholy panic. Fear whispered along her spine.

'Your cheeks are very flushed,' he said conversationally. 'I can feel the heat off your skin.'

'My blood boils very easily.'

'That makes two of us.'

'You're forgetting I'm used to you,' she said breathlessly.

'Are you?' he asked sardonically. 'You weren't even certain of your welcome, that's how much you know about me.'

'I know you do the most dreadful, unexpected things!'

'Not at all. This has been years coming. I'm tired of the masquerade anyway.'

'Don't you dare experiment on me!' she cried out, exasperated.

'Even you, Giannina, know when your number is up!'

'*Please*, Ingo!' she held up a staying hand, touching his cheek. 'I apologise for everything I've ever done. I've forgotten what it was.'

'*I* haven't, but I'll accept your apology for what it's worth. The thing is, Giannina, you can't stop what's happening. In fact, you have no choice in the matter. Give in gracefully, seeing there's no escape.'

Her fingers clenched convulsively on his, vainly trying to soothe him, but he forced her head back, holding it in position, her soft mouth parted with the slight, painful jerk on her silky curls. 'You'll be sorry!' she promised him wrathfully, her true nature emerging, her dark eyes flashing in her cameo face.

He only laughed, anticipating her struggles, holding her still. Then with marvellous insolence he bent his dark head and barely brushed her mouth with his own. Just a shiver of feeling, yet its shock was as complete as a ravishment. Genny let out her breath, trembling violently, seeing him as the ultimate tormentor, driven to playing this cat-and-mouse game with her. Strong feelings were deep-running within her—not love, nor hate, but something in between. She wasn't

Ingo's plaything, but her own woman and all her old antagonisms began to wash up like a tidal wave. He had his own special way of triggering off her violent moods, almost as if he enjoyed them, his hands pinning her wrists with an unconquerable strength.

Still she struggled, fiercely, but oddly mechanically, as if she had been long since programmed to be at war with him. She was blind to the beautiful, bewitching stars, the fragrant soft purple peace of the night. 'You don't know what you want, do you?' he ground out, lifting her with one perfect, flowing movement right across his knees.

'You think you can do anything you like!' she raged at him, her voice breaking pathetically and her eyes shining with tears.

'I'm only doing what we're both craving!'

He found her mouth with an unbearable passion, a fierce kind of necessity that made her heart give a great bound, quivering in her breast like a mad thing. The shock was so tumultuous that her mouth parted of its own accord under that wild questing, a punishment as driving as it was darkly relentless. She could feel her body go limp against him, a small moan escaping her that made him loosen his cruel hold. Her small head was thrown back against his shoulder and he lifted her even closer to him, deliberately, his hand curving over her breast to feel her heart storming into his palm.

There was no respite, only a boundless excitement, a wild passion that incited Genny's body and arrested her mind, so that in a very short time she began to respond from the depths of her tempestuous nature, pierced by this miracle of sensation. The hunger and urgency he was creating in her was obtrusive now, demanding much more than the deep intoxication of

67

caresses, the hard ecstasy of his mouth. Given her head she was showing a breathtaking response that afterwards would make her writhe with shame, a fire whipped up by his devastating masculinity. Whatever kisses she had invited before in her life, they were totally banished from her mind. No other feeling compared with this one. She had been no more than an untutored child, yet Ingo was holding her as though he loved kissing her, unsatiated by the assault on her soft mouth, the feel of her body flowing like silk against him.

It was insane for so many reasons, as though both of them were forbidden the other. Nothing was real to her, least of all her own surrender. It was Ingo who broke away, cutting off the enravishment so completely that Genny knew an incurable resentment. She opened her eyes, so close to him that she couldn't focus on his face. 'Oh, glory!' she said in a shattered kind of voice.

'Sorry, baby, it's not a good idea to stay here.'

'Why not? Where else do the cymbals clang and the drums go bang? One of us is crazy, possibly both.'

'Settle for me. My desire for you knows no bounds.'

'Well, I must be the last one to know it!' She drew a drowsy breath, almost spent. 'Tell me, O Mighty One, how are we going to hurdle this latest disaster?'

'Easy. Keep on remembering what it did to us. Daylight always brings better sense anyway.'

'I can't believe it!' she persisted, still relaxed against him. 'I don't even feel my body is my own.'

'I understand completely,' he said dryly.

'I'd say this was adding insult to injury!'

'You've been kissed before,' he murmured laconically.

'That was my best to date. I'll undoubtedly come back for more.'

'I can't promise anything with any certainty. I've got work to do. I can't have a curly-headed girl-child coming between me and Tandarro.'

She stared up at the stars swinging dizzily, feeling the old familiar uprising, instant transformation. When the shafts of magic were over they were back to square one again. 'Is this any way to treat me after all these years?' she snapped.

'I'm wondering now why I waited. On the first try no room for improvement? I have to consider now if you could respond like that to another man.'

'Suppose I said I could and I do!'

'Then I'd strangle you right here and now.'

'I'd rather die before I let you!'

He turned her face about, a light finger on her chin. 'You're not going to moan about it, are you, baby? My motive was the finest, to further your education. What could be purer than that?'

'I was very content the way I was, thank you!'

'Such a shame you've taken to lying.' He moved his hand a little, tracing her profile. 'What an exquisite mouth you have. It nearly sent me into shock.'

'Perhaps it was mutual, which is very odd indeed,' she said, puzzled.

'Unfortunately I can't bring myself to kiss you again. Once is enough.'

'I've never taken to drugs, so why should I take to your kisses? So far as I'm concerned that was an unforgettable experience, better over.'

'I'll see you keep to that!' he said briskly.

'Then you might let me up.'

'Sure you don't want me to kiss you again?' He came to his feet in one lithe co-ordinated movement, bringing her up with him.

'Dave's coming next week,' she announced, swaying. 'I can wait until then.'

'You'll be able to show him an improvement.'

'That's my business.'

'You could thank me.'

'I won't fall into that trap. You might think it permissible to take things a step further. It's ironic, though, isn't it?'

He put out a hand, steadying her. 'What is?'

'The hurdles, the snags, the mighty rapids. A man like you could wash me away—name, personality, aims and ambitions. Nothing but a nothing. A Faulkner possession.'

'Giannina, you can't be serious?'

'*You're* never serious!'

'Maybe I don't want you to know how badly I want you. You're too young and you still go to school. You're even a cousin of sorts. You know how people talk!'

Genny pouted. 'No one talks like you! I wish you'd just go away.'

'That's the only thing I won't do,' retorted Ingo. 'Think you can make it up the bank?'

She smacked his hand away, fighting for her self-possession, hearing his mocking:

'Dave ride?'

'He's a professional man,' she answered shortly.

'I said, does Dave ride?'

'Actually he doesn't. He's a doctor.'

'I won't hold that against him,' he opined. 'You could teach him, of course, though that'd be real suicide if you want my opinion. Maybe you'd prefer me to do it.'

She clenched her small white teeth, breaking into a run. 'From this minute on, I'm going to ignore you.'

'It might be best at that. Has Dave got any money?'

'How should I know? I've never asked him.'

By the time she reached the horses Genny was puffing and Ingo wasn't even out of breath. 'I can't understand that, Giannina,' he said, picking up the conversation. 'You've lived very well up to date. Take my advice and check him out. You want to be certain he can support you in the manner to which you've become accustomed.'

70

'Hughie wasn't rich,' she burst out, as though she had to explain herself, 'just comfortable. Of course Flick still has money of her own, but I won't miss a few luxuries. We've never had the likes of Tandarro, you know. Even to build the house at today's prices would clean a millionaire out.'

'One thing at a time, Genny!' he said, quietening her. 'I'm glad you've invited Dave out. You didn't ask me, but I'm still glad. It will gave me the opportunity to act as your closest male relative, in this country at any rate. I suppose you have a score of relatives in Italy, not to speak of half-sisters and brothers. Carlo was only a young man when Flick threw him out. I'll see if this Dave of yours is suitable, ready and willing and able to support you. I just hope he knows you're a handful. Most men would find it scary!'

'Doctor's don't scare easily,' she said repressively.

'There's that, of course, but they've nothing on their minds but stomach-aches and allergies. Why on earth should you insist on marrying someone so unromantic?'

'He's romantic enough for me. It's *you* who ought to be ashamed of yourself,' she snapped back.

'I'm not!' he said, laughing.

'Then you damned well ought to be.'

He gave her a leg up on to the colt, seeing her seated and holding the reins. 'No one set a monstrous trap for you, Giannina.'

'I suppose you're right,' she agreed grudgingly. 'Don't expect me to admit it in the morning.'

He grinned. 'A deal! I won't even remember it. I'm showing Dan around the property on a motorbike. Think of the spills!'

She laughed, but it wasn't really a happy sound. His arrogant dark head was tilted up to her, his beautiful mouth twisted with humour. 'A loner by choice!' she

71

said rather sadly. 'Don't think I'm out to threaten you, Ingo Faulkner. So far as I'm concerned you can go to your grave a bachelor, incapable of letting anyone get close to you.'

'Now that's funny coming from you, or are you going to say I took unfair advantage of you?' he demanded.

'No, we'll stick to the facts.'

'That's my girl.'

'Don't go thinking that!' she exclaimed. 'I consider myself as independent as you are.'

'It's everything, flower face! Forget what you feel like in my arms.'

'Don't expect to have me there again.'

'Why must you throw out these challenges?' He whistled up the stallion and lifted himself into the saddle. 'No man is wholly predictable, especially on starry nights. Let's go home and see if Flick is thinking of changing her address.'

'Don't say it!' Genny shivered, channelling her thought into another direction. 'I'm over-anxious as it is.'

'Hadn't you better pay attention to your own problem?' inquired Ingo.

'Which is?'

'Why expect me to give you the answers?'

'You've never avoided saying your piece in the past. Vociferously, actually!'

'There's a word!' he gibed.

'I've never had any difficulty with languages,' Genny sniffed.

'Well, you don't swear as you used to.'

'What would you expect with so many stockmen around?'

'You weren't supposed to be there at the time,' he said dryly.

'I like lots of colour, excitement and danger!'

'*No* news!' Ingo said ironically.

'You don't have to be so sarcastic. How's the scratch?' she asked briskly.

'I'll get Doctor Dave to take a look at it.'

'It will be all healed over by the time he gets here.'

'Which I might as well hear about now. When is he due?'

'Some time Friday, for a week. Ginger will fly him in,' Genny answered levelly.

'Who's taking care of the patients, or do they do better on their own?'

'He's taking a week's leave from the hospital!' she said with a semblance of politeness. 'He's not in private practice yet.'

'What a pity, I'm sure the outside world would benefit.'

'Flick likes him.'

He gave a spurt of laughter full of amused irony. 'It would be very odd if she didn't. I assume he's a personable young man, clean-cut, with nice manners and just a dash of mischief!'

'For God's sake, Ingo!' she said.

'What's the matter?' His silvery eyes in the night were gleaming like a cat's.

She passed a hand across her brow. 'I feel odd. I even think I could cry.'

'You never cry except in a rage,' he said.

'I'm in a kind of rage now.'

'Maybe you're just on the verge of self-discovery.'

'*Mamma mia*, it's rugged!' she groaned.

His white smile was brilliant, friendly and relaxed. 'You owe it to yourself, Giannina, to make the effort.'

They had been riding side by side through the exhilarating night, the horses walking sedately, treading delicately across the endless plains country. Now Genny drew away, apparently deep in thought. The silence went on for some little time with the fragrant air swirling around them, ruffling Genny's short curls into a shining halo. Ingo reined in beside her and leaned forward a little in the saddle so he could stare into her eyes.

'What's on your mind?'

'You can't imagine!' she returned.

'*Tell* me.' He caught hold of the reins.

'I've decided it was an unspeakable mistake for you to kiss me.'

'Really? I thought it was terrific.'

'Then I'm suffering on my own.'

'Oh well!' He shrugged his wide shoulders, his gaze sparkling and deliberate. 'Who put the idea into my head in the first place?'

'From which I gather I'm supposed to take the blame?'

'Exactly. Eve is still a lady!'.

Genny wanted desperately to see his true expression, but it was too dark, all she could see was the mocking glitter in his eyes. She threw up her head with a certain amount of bravado. 'I'm disappointed in you, Ingo. I didn't think any woman could tempt you.'

'None better than you, kiddo!' he teased.

'What a triumph!'

'Just don't tell anybody.'

'What about Sally?' she demanded.

'It would utterly throw her.'

'I know. She has lots of plans.'

'That won't do her the least bit of good.' Ingo smiled.

'Then why don't you damned well tell her?' Genny demanded, her hostility rising.

'I'm certain she wouldn't listen to anything I have to say. You know women!'

'We both know that you do!'

'What's that supposed to mean?'

'Skip it. You're a terrible man! If I didn't love it out here so much, you wouldn't see me for dust. This must be the best part of the world, Tandarro!'

'I think so,' he said, and his black velvet voice had pride and possession in it, a bred-in-the-bone arrogance.

'Yet it takes lives,' Gerry said softly. 'It took your father's. It takes all your time, all your energies. It's so *big*! I suppose it might make Dave just that bit nervous.'

'Is there any good reason for that?' he asked rather impatiently.

'Why, how *rich* you are, stupid! The homestead and the immense size of the property,' she explained in surprise. 'Surely you can see it? Though I suppose you mightn't. You've been used to it all your life. Dave's jaw will just drop open, I know. Even Dan was struck all of a heap by the Faulkner idea of comfort!'

'I don't think he has any idea of copying it, and who said you could call me stupid?'

'I avoid all the usual words other people apply to you.'

'So I've noticed.' Ingo's voice was grim. 'I can guarantee you're the only one that's come up with that one.'

'It's very ordinary. Still, I'm sensible it doesn't really apply to you. It's Dave who's going to look silly with his mouth open for a day or two.'

'As long as he doesn't faint dead away!' Ingo said crisply. 'Surely he comes from a pleasant environment?'

'Very pleasant, but this is grandeur. If you don't know, I can't explain. This is your home and therefore taken for granted.'

'Wrong, it's my passion,' he corrected.

'Yes,' she said sombrely, 'you're a very formidable man and your power is real.'

'I don't abuse it, Giannina.'

'You sound angry.'

75

'I'm not. A bit browned off, maybe. You're no stranger to our way of life. You know the set-up. What I say goes out here and it *has* to, but no one is a second-class citizen on this station. Any kind of power entails responsibility. Sometimes you even get the worst of the bargain, so much is expected. Despite all the discussions no one really likes making the decisions. Too much is involved. That's my job—if I'm everyone's boss then I have to be sure I'm the right kind of man to follow.'

'And you are!' she said, leaning her head on his shoulder, only half fooling, the other half very serious. 'We're all yours, Ingo Faulkner, only please take good care of me.'

'What other kind of care have you known?' he asked tersely. 'It's common knowledge, cherub, that you've been spoilt rotten.'

'Not true!' she said heatedly, lifting her head.

'That's the worst of it, women can dish it out, but they can't take it. A stormy past and a stormy future is all I can expect of you.'

'What else do you want, damn it, to *own* me?'

'It might be better that way!'

Genny was furious. 'Really, you're power mad! Just listen to me, Ingo, I know what kind of man you are. I know everyone around here worships the very ground you walk upon, and why shouldn't they? You support every one of them right down to the last little piccaninny, but I'm different. You might have the right to call thousands of square miles your own, but like it or not, I'm not and never will be your property!'

'You were very convincing ten minutes ago,' he averred. 'I could have sworn you were made for me. Come on, let's get riding. This is going to take some time, I can see.'

'What is?' she said, urging the colt on.

'Breaking you in. Still, one can't have it both ways. I like plenty of spirit even if it's hard to control it.'

'Yes, because you're really a very violent man. It's not the first time I've thought it. You fascinate me. All that perfect public manner, that classy way you have about you is nothing but a veneer. You're nothing but a savage!'

'Just how savage you've yet to find out,' he told her, 'and you will. Probably your first real taste of reality ...'

'You don't alarm me!' she said recklessly, with an inbuilt penchant for calamity.

'And I'm not going to take any notice of you either. Not for now. When we get back I'm going to have a few neat whiskies. I feel an overpowering need for it.'

'Then let's get back where you belong!' Genny almost shouted at him, all the tension of the earlier part of the day back on her again. She touched the colt's glossy sides, and it sprang away, surging ahead. Now for the first time, Tandarro seemed too big, too unconquerable. Too hostile to women.

She rode as fast as she could and even as she hurdled the fence of the compound the stallion flashed by her, completely confident, suspended for a second, its powerful hind legs tucked well up, its magnificent head and neck stretched to the fullest limit before it came down on the other side, one front leg a little in advance of the other. Red Dust, the only horse on the station she was forbidden to ride. Genny made for the stables, taking good care to keep out of Ingo's way.

CHAPTER FOUR

GENNY was nearing the holding yards before Dan caught up with her and together, their conversation friendly and lighthearted, they made their way towards the big fenced paddock where a herd of brumbies awaited the breaking-in process. It was only early, yet already it was very hot, the sky above them an amazing dense blue with not a cloud anywhere. Birds exploded from the branches of the trees about them, chattering wildly, hundreds and hundreds of green budgerigars, wheeling and diving in their characteristic faultless formation, their wings in the sun with a brilliant sheen of emerald, and almost as many rose-pink galahs and the big black cockatoos with their gorgeous red tail feathers and their curious calls, the fluttering little crimson chats and the zebra finches, and much higher up, soaring, the predators, the eagles and the hawks.

Dan, staring up, stumbled and Genny couldn't help laughing. Dan laughed too, holding up his arms to all the living beauty around him. 'This is kinda dazzling, isn't it?'

'That's everyone's reaction,' smiled Genny. 'The Outback is famous for its bird life. Gigantic flocks are commonplace. The Channel Country is a major breeding ground, especially for water birds. When all the channels and the billabongs are full, the birds move in in their countless thousands. They're nomadic, they have to be, and they turn up overnight. The pelican colonies are the only ones you might have to go searching for. They nest in the remote swamps, but they come out when the waterholes start drying up. There are huge flocks of ibis down in the lignum swamps; spoonbills, shags, herons, the whistling tree duck. They're

78

really wild and tremendously alert. All the perky little birds, the budgies and the finches and the wrens are so prolific not even the hawks and the falcons can finish them off.'

She continued, 'If you want to come down to the river I can show you coolibahs covered in corellas like huge white flowers. I don't know how they can even find a stand on a branch, there are so many of them. If you clap your hands and startle them they fly off all together, leaving the tree green again. Then we have the glorious enamelled beauties, the parrots. We love our birds and protect them, but people like to pinch them, you know. They sell for quite a price overseas. It's illegal, of course, to trap our beautiful parrots, but bird dealers make quick profits out of the constant demand for cage birds. The Golden Shoulder from Cape York Peninsula can fetch up to three thousand dollars in Europe. The fact that the bird is protected doesn't seem to bother the smugglers. They drug the birds and get them out one way or the other. Some are caught. Nothing serious, just a threat to the survival of a bird of great beauty. I'd like to see anyone trying to trap our birds. Ingo would skin them alive.'

'And that I can understand!' Dan said, chuckling. 'This is almost a sanctuary.'

'Not almost. It is!' Genny said quite seriously, her small face shadowed by her black gaucho hat. In the shimmering dry heat, the mirage was skeining silvery lagoons across the flower-fringed plains. It was a sight that made Genny's blood tingle, an entrancing vision that could 'fill a man's vision or crush him,' Ingo had once said. In the good seasons, in the flower-scented air, it was Paradise itself, but this immense Eden could change into something frightful in times of drought. That Genny knew well. This was a land of harsh extremes, from the grim aridity of the desiccated plains

79

littered with the bleached bones of dead cattle, to the jewel-like never-ending carpets of wild flowers that sprang miraculously from the red soil after the rain.

But whatever the setbacks, the searing tragedies of flood and drought and personal disaster, it was the end of the rainbow for the men like Ingo, descendants of the great pioneering families who had made monumental treks of distance and hardship, living with the land and gaining strength from it had become a tradition, with a man's pride and sense of oneness with his environment very assured and apparent. The women went with their men, not so at home perhaps in such splendid isolation and surrounded by dangers, but they learned to accept this challenging way of life and very often came to love it. Others found the loneliness unbearable, the fear of sickness and accident, the life and death threats to their children without medical attention at hand. Two great innovations had changed all that—the Flying Doctor service and the huge radio service that linked up the vast outback. The School of the Air then came into operation, providing an education for the homestead children who weren't sent away to the boarding schools in the cities. On the big stations that maintained light aircraft for their personal use, distance was conquered. Flying to one's destination had become as everyday as the city's commuter taking a bus or a train.

Dan was busy looking all about him, finding something of interest everywhere, his deep drawl and dry humour falling pleasantly on Genny's ears. Station hands at work on their various jobs called a greeting to him with warmth in it and Dan returned it, taking for granted the nice, easy camaraderie common to the male of the species. In common, too, with the rest of the men, he wore jeans and a bush shirt and high stockman's boots, the only difference being the creamy perfection of his ten-gallon hat. After about fifteen minutes down at the yards the Stetson began to look more realistic, speckled with red dust and adjusted to a more protective angle.

Genny was dressed for riding as well in jeans and an easy shirt in blue cotton denim with a red scarf tucked inside, the soft colour of her shirt matching the wide leather belt around her narrow waist. Her dark eyes were sparkling with youthful vitality, the healthy colour a soft bloom under her skin. Dan considered she looked perfect, comfortable and easy and unmistakably feminine. He would liked to have seen Felicity in just such a get-up. Actually he would have liked to have just seen Felicity. He found it hard to understand, but he couldn't get Felicity off his mind. She was a most interesting woman and she looked barely more than a child.

'Where's Miss Felicity this mornin'?' he asked artlessly.

Genny smiled, just waiting for the question. 'Flick always sleeps late, and you'd never find her down here in any case. Not with all this dust flying and so much exhausting action.'

Dan studied her closely for a moment. 'You don't look very much like your mother.'

'No contest,' Genny said, still smiling.

'I can't think when I've seen two prettier women.'

'Not even approximately, Dan?' she teased.

'Maybe on the screen. I'll tell you one thing, Miss Felicity looks a girl!'

'Doesn't she now.'

'Hope I didn't bore her last night. I guess I talked and talked about just about everything!'

'Flick's a very good listener,' agreed Genny.

'You got it! A very understanding woman, and she looks a picture. Funny, being a bachelor for so long I usually tend to freeze in a woman's company, but I never felt one jittery minute with your mother. God knows why I didn't, but I didn't. She being so beautiful and all, it kinda makes a man tongue-tied.'

'I'm sure you don't need to worry about holding a woman's attention, Dan. You're a very interesting man.'

'Can't shut me up in company. It's just when I'm on my own. Being a bachelor has done that to me. My mother was eighty-eight when she died; she was my guiding star.'

'Did she live with you, Dan?'

Dan nodded. 'Yes, ma'am, and a wiser head I've never found. You'd have loved her. She used to glare at me and say: "Why the hell don't you come home with a bride?" It used to annoy her that I was the only one of her flock not to raise a family of my own. Took practically all my time building up the ranch. I figure I'll think about it now. Seems hardly fair now she's gone.'

'Keep a cool head, Dan!' Genny warned. 'Marriage isn't all it's cracked up to be, really!'

'And how would you know, miss?' he asked.

'I've done a lot of observing!' Genny said dryly, seeing from the expression on Dan's face that he had indeed done all the talking the night before. It was Flick's pattern to let a man get in too deep before she volunteered any information, like her three marriages. It seemed a pity to upset Dan's plans, but Felicity was as irresponsible as a child. Love was always just around the corner and Dan had a right to be warned.

'There now!' Dan moved a little closer, his face puzzled. 'You being an only child you'd barely know anything else but a happy home life.'

'That doesn't follow, Dan. I'm afraid very many "only children" have an unsatisfactory time of it. Worse and yet worse, Dan, there's quite a bit Flick hasn't told you.'

'Couldn't be anything a woman like Miss Felicity would have to hide!' he protested.

'True, Dan, only one or two unusual things.'

'Such as?' Dan asked, smiling, and faintly talking down to her.

'Flick's been married three times.'

Dan flushed under his ruddy tan and made a valiant bid to swallow whatever exclamation rose to his throat.

'Yes, three times,' Genny said calmly.

'Whatever happened to all of them?' Dan finally asked.

'Two Flick divorced, the first my father, and the last one died. Maybe she would have stayed with Hughie for ever, but there you are, that's what happened. Are you so very surprised?'

'Yes and no,' he admitted.

'Is it going to make a difference, Dan?' asked Genny. 'I know you find Flick a very attractive woman. She would have got round to telling you, of course.'

'One marriage would be enough for me,' Dan mumbled, rather stricken. 'Sorry, sorry, no offence meant.'

'And none taken, Dan. Perhaps you think I had no business telling you?'

'No, no, I wanted to know. Miss Felicity never said a word.'

'Well, you've only just met her, Dan, but sometimes a climax can come at the beginning. I just acted on impulse in telling you. You see, I have a feeling you may influence Flick's life and I love her dearly.'

'And what did ... Hughie, was it, die of?' Dan asked, almost speaking to himself.

'Natural causes. Flick was devastated. She was really very fond of him, in fact she went so far down in health that she had me really worried. Ingo insisted she come out here to be looked after. He's always looked after her.'

'He's a very refined gentleman,' Dan said vaguely.

'You look disappointed, Dan, shocked,' said Genny.

'No. You see, Genny, I like everything about your mother. Maybe not the fact that she's had three husbands—any woman I married would have to stay well and truly put. I make no secret of the fact that she put the idea of settling down into my mind. I appreciate honesty.'

'Dan,' Genny said firmly, 'Flick would have told you all the bits and pieces by herself, but you and I understand one another and I wanted you to be prepared. Flick is special, but she does need looking after and I've been doing that for quite a while. The events of her life are my life. I don't want you to hurt her, nor do I want her to hurt you. It's possible if we keep this our secret no one will be hurt. Flick can be very compelling...'

'Like magic!' Dan supplied. 'Those innocent blue eyes!'

'They are innocent,' confirmed Genny.

'Maybe she never met the right man,' he said thoughtfully.

'She's had more chance than most. Flirtation is a way of life to Flick. I suppose she would be like one of your southern belles. She's fragile and tender and she wants only to be happy.'

'Yes, she's precious all right!' Dan said, resilient as a whip. 'She lacks solidity, stability, and that the right man can supply.'

'If you think so, Dan!' Genny said rather wearily, realising that the expression on Dan's face was defying common sense. Well, she had done her bit. Flick wouldn't have told him until he was well and truly hooked and Ingo wouldn't have interfered in any way. Flick had made another conquest—it was written all over Dan's dreaming face. Time was as nothing when

84

attraction occurred. Perhaps Dan would be the start of something big or he would fly away into oblivion. With her highly cultivated sixth sense, Genny was convinced that Dan was already written down in the pages of Flick's diary. She shouldn't worry, Flick was a grown woman, but she did. She had never liked merry-go-rounds. They made her dizzy.

In the holding paddock Billy Swan, the half-caste horse-breaker, was herding his high-spirited, nervous charges. They raced in wide circles around the yard, churning up great clouds of red dust, their whinnies loud with fright and anger, their manes and tails streaming in the wind of their own unbridled motion. Genny moved to the fence of the adjoining yard, climbed up on it and tucked her boots under the rails.

'Sure you're safe up there, honey?' Dan asked.

'I am until Ingo shows up!' she rejoined.

'Where is he?' Dan asked, joining her.

'I've no idea. Ingo gets up with the birds.'

'So do I when I'm at home. Just look at that leader. He looks vicious!'

'He sure does!' Genny looked to where a big, high-mettled wild horse, black in colour with a white blaze and one white sock, was whirling about, ready to break from the herd and charge Billy. Billy met this frightening dynamic charge with amazing calm, sidestepping neatly with a natural dancer's grace, as he prepared to land a lasso around the brumby's neck.

The rope fell with accuracy and the horse reared and bucked, then continued its mad careering around the yard with the slight Billy holding on for dear life to the rope that slid in lengths through his heavily-gloved hands. Separated from the mob, their leader was now selected to have his magnificent independence broken down; the rest of them driven back into the neighbouring yard, screamed defiance, urging their leader to resist and resist these ruthless humans.

'It's kinda sad, isn't it?' said Dan, the cattleman.

'Billy's good and he's not cruel. He really loves those horses. That selfsame stallion is going to turn into a good working horse, strong and dependable.' Genny shrugged. 'I suppose it's unnatural in a way to try and break his proud spirit. No wonder he looks so enraged.'

'He'll grow tired of it soon. Kinda like a kid in school.'

As Billy was working quite a few of the stockmen climbed up on to the fence to tell Billy to: 'Watch it!' After a minute or so Genny and Dan found themselves adding their cautions. Horse power was frightening. One kick from those flying hooves would settle Billy, yet he moved closer and closer to the terrified animal, slowly reaching out a hand and caressing its sweating neck. A stream of soft patter was issuing from his mouth, the most incredible mixture of English and dialect and indistinct swearing, all delivered at a low crooning chant. From the other side, Billy's assistant Lofty, a predictable beanpole, moved as silently as any shadow, coming up with the bridle and manoeuvring it until like a miracle it was over the stallion's head with the bit in its mouth.

'The first step!' said Dan quietly. 'Probably it'll chew on it like a baby with its dummy!'

True enough, instead of rearing madly, or trying to spit this strange object out, the stallion accepted the bit and began to chew rhythmically, exploring this not unpleasant new sensation. Billy continued patting and crooning while Lofty very stealthily began fixing the hobbling chains, rendering the animal almost powerless. Another minute more and the stallion tried to move its legs, apparently without suspicion that anything had been done to it. All hell broke loose.

Genny whipped off her silk scarf and tied it round her nose and mouth like a small bandit. The dust was flying as the stallion endeavoured to rear and buck, the chains clanging, its eyes savage and distended; it foamed at the mouth, starting to stumble around and around with the violence of impotence. Its brothers in the yard beyond wheeled and snorted and kicked up their hind legs in sympathy.

'That's a very strong horse!' Dan said unnecessarily.

'I hope he'll be quiet soon,' answered Genny. 'His heart must be fit to burst.'

Billy, awaiting just such a moment, was leaning nonchalantly back against the fence, smoking his pipe. When the horse was exhausted, he closed in on the slobbering animal, patting it affectionately, calling it congratulatory names, then hauled the gear off before slapping it on the rump and sending it off through the gate Lofty opened into the fenced paddock beyond. 'That'll do 'im for today! Send in the next one!'

Dan on the fence was curbing the wild urge to have a go himself. Though he had been handling horses all his life he had never used wild horses on his ranch. He could ride like a vaquero and he had ridden many a buck-jumper in his younger days. A thought occurred to him.

'Ask Billy if he's got one,' he asked Genny suddenly.

'Got what?' she inquired.

'A wild one. A mustang. I've got a powerful urge to ride one.'

'Take it easy, boss!' Billy warned laconically, with ears that could hear a leaf drop.

'You're good, boy,' Dan called, 'but I'm not too bad myself!'

'Come on then, Billy, what are you waiting for?' Lofty yelled, looking up at the fence at Dan with some favour. Not a stockman among them would hesitate to expose themselves to outrageous danger in the name of entertainment, so Dan's yen to ride a buck-jumper didn't seem at all out of the way. Still Billy hesitated, not so much thinking of Dan or possible injury but of what the Boss would say. He had a week to break in this mob, but he had a little time up his sleeve. If the big Texan wanted a few thrills, why not? He just had to be a good rider coming from the part of the world. 'Course he was a little old to take a bad spill, but no one could tell a man he was too old to try his hand at anything he fancied, least of all Billy. His liquid black eyes ranged over to the far yard searching out the piebald mare— a contrary piece. She looked like nothing, but she could deflate the toughest ego.

'Don't do anything foolish, Dan!' Genny counselled. Woman-like, she was unable to keep out of it.

'What have you got in mind, Billy?' Dan asked, not even hearing her.

'Only a little piebald somethin'. Wouldn't attempt to ride 'er meself, boss!'

'Had a saddle on her?' Dan asked.

'Sure, it's the riders that come off. Lofty, jus' yesterday. She's just naturally wild like all females. Maybe we'd better wait for the boss.'

'Why, Ingo wouldn't give a damn!' Dan exclaimed, slapping his thigh with satisfaction. 'Why, he told me to treat the station like my own and *I* say I wanna ride!'

'Whacko!' shouted the men enjoyably.

'Turn the bay out,' Billy ordered, 'and bring in the piebald. The placid little lady in the far paddock.'

Dan glanced back at Genny, his eyes shining, while she just sat there pondering the probable outcome. It was out of her control. She could hardly tell him to stop; men didn't take kindly to a woman's intervention and superior wisdom. Besides, she had no desire to offend him. She had said quite enough for the morning.

A man like Dan, probably born in the saddle, surely didn't need supervision. Lofty was leading in the saddled-up mare, a bag tied over its unprepossessing head. It was walking quietly enough, even sedately.

'Lassiter's Last Ride!' one of the boys called out, breaking up with laughter.

Dan turned and shook a huge fist at him, not knowing Lassiter, but correctly surmising he had come to grief.

'He's dead game 'orright!' Lofty pronounced, while Dan hauled himself into the saddle in one flowing movement, an expert horseman.

'Ride 'em, cowboy!' they all yelled in a chorus, really surprised that Dan was still in the saddle.

The mare stood with Dan's big frame astride it as though it was posing for a picture. Dan too seemed glued there, his hips and his shoulders stiff. Genny felt the colour come into her face. Men made no sense at all! Why would Dan want to risk injury, especially now when he was thinking of marriage? Her lips began to move soundlessly. The piebald was a rogue and incredibly cunning. Half the staff seemed to have arrived, though the piebald didn't appear in the least inclined to gratify the grandstand. Dan gave it a little nudge along and it laid its ears back, the only indication that it wasn't having a nice time. Dan, beginning to suspect a hoax, now put a little more weight into the side kick and the piebald took off like a mule, its tail clamped down between its hind legs, bucking in earnest, moving like a rocket to the opposite side of the fence.

A pair of arms reached up and hauled Genny clean off the fence with a kind of cold fury, holding her well back, silver eyes intent on the age-old spectacle, man bent on riding a savagely bucking horse. Dan, he was certain, could count on being thrown, though he was as tough as old leather and highly experienced, anticipating every move the piebald thought up. The dust was swirling, streaking the stockmen's faces, starting to look a little anxious now, having caught sight of the boss. Now for the first time it seemed to occur to them that, though the big Texan was good, he wasn't a young man like Billy and he was tiring. Those powerful jerks on his arms and his spine would have broken a lesser man. The contest was taking its toll and the piebald still had plenty of energy in hand.

Genny, hauled back hard under Ingo's shoulder, could feel the silent rage in him. The piebald, certain now that its rider was weakening, started out on a series of risings and plungings that ricocheted Dan out the saddle and hard on to the red dust. He came down with a jarring thud on his right side and lay there.

'Get that bloody nag!' Ingo shouted in a voice that brought every last man off the fence.

Genny, terrified that Dan would be stamped on, broke away from the lightened lock on her and rushed to the fence, climbed it and jumped to the other side, ignoring Ingo's tense shout that galvanised them all into action, waving and shooing the mare into a corner where Billy, driven to try almost anything, jumped on the piebald's back and rode it away.

So far as Dan was concerned it was the final insult. He lay there groaning, nursing his shoulder, his pride and his collar-bone fractured. Genny's lovely anxious face swam into view and he tried to smile at her.

'Where does it hurt?' She touched his scraped cheek gently. 'That was a marvellous ride, but oh, Dan!'

For the second time Ingo just lifted her bodily away, dropping to his haunches and running practised hands over Dan's jarred limbs. 'Nothing broken!' he reported tersely. 'Nothing important anyway, just your collar-bone.'

'Now see here, boy, no one forced me,' Dan said.

'I know. Can you get up?'

'Sure. Gimme a minute first, I'm kinda winded. Did you see that goddam Billy ride the thing away?'

'It was nearly finished,' replied Ingo.

'I'm not the man I used to be!' Dan exclaimed, full of self-disgust. 'I wouldn't rightly know how I'm going to live this down.'

'We promise not to tell anyone,' Ingo said a little grimly. 'You could have broken your neck. You were lucky!'

'I tell you that piebald was going like it was possessed!' Dan looked past Ingo's dark face to Genny. 'Hey, you're not feeling sorry for me are you, Genny?'

'She'll be feeling sorry for herself before she gets back to the house!' Ingo answered shortly.

'But I'm feeling fine! Help me up.'

'I'll be glad to.'

'There you go!' said Dan, turning noticeably white.

'Are you all right, Dan?' Genny said anxiously.

Ingo turned to her, his silvery eyes frosty. 'Move the jeep up here and we'll settle Dan in it. The keys are still in it. Go on, *move*! You're pretty good at flying into danger, now you can't tear yourself away.'

'All right, I'm going!'

'Don't upset her,' Dan said, regarding Ingo intently. 'You sound like you might cut a switch off a tree, and she sure is one pretty little girl. Tender-hearted too!'

Ingo didn't reply. With the sun glaring down on Dan's face it was plain that he was in a lot of pain. Lofty advanced rather diffidently with Dan's Stetson, bringing it down on the seat of his pants.

'Good to see you on your feet. What's that bone stickin' out?' he inquired.

'That's his collar-bone,' Ingo supplied in a dampening tone. 'If you haven't got any better plans in mind, why don't you go back to the brumbies?'

91

'Goin', boss!' Lofty said with a minimum of words.

The ride over, everyone seemed to have dispersed with remarkable speed. Genny brought the jeep right up to the yards, opening the door while Dan got himself into the passenger seat with a little assistance. 'Haven't had an accident in thirty years!' he said, grinning wryly.

'You'll feel better with a good stiff drink inside you,' Genny promised, climbing over into the back seat without being told. Although Ingo was pretty good about a lot of things he didn't for a moment consider being driven by a woman. One had to accept the bitter pills with the sweet talk, and there would be no sweet talk today. Besides, she hadn't been in any real danger. Lofty and a few of the boys had been getting hold of the piebald just as she landed inside the yard. As usual she had acted on impulse, and one look at Ingo's face made her sure she was in for a lecture. Dan turned back to look at her, wincing a little.

'Don't worry!' he whispered like a conspirator.

She smiled at him and caught Ingo's eyes in the rear vision mirror, very cool and determined. A fitful breeze had sprung up, blowing through her curls and the collar of her shirt. The red silk bandana hung down in the opening and she turned it round the right way, retying it in a chic knot around her throat.

'All right, Ingo,' she said lightly, 'you can deliver your lecture now.'

'I'll do that when there's no one around to hear you cry out.'

'You surely don't think it was young Genny's fault!' Dan cried, surprised but ready to rush to Genny's defence.

'Not at all!' Ingo said suavely. 'What you didn't see, Dan, being flat on your back, was Genny diving away from me and into the ring before the boys had the piebald under control. Moments like that give a man heart failure. I've had plenty of scares in my time, mostly on Genny's account. She has a reckless streak I only occasionally enjoy!'

'I'm impulsive, maybe!' Genny said flippantly. 'I've never aspired to be reckless.'

'Either way it depresses me.'

'Maddens you, you mean!'

'That too!'

Genny shrugged off his hard tone. 'Flick will be upset,' she announced for Dan's benefit.

'About *me*?' Dan asked, considerably cheered.

'Just wait and see.'

'If it's going to upset her, maybe we shouldn't tell her!' Dan said manfully.

'We'll *have* to. You haven't caught sight of yourself yet.'

'I'm not disfigured, am I, ma'am?'

'No, you look like the returning hero. Your collar bone is sticking out and the right side of your face is cut up a bit, otherwise you look great!'

'When we get back,' Ingo said quietly, breaking in on Genny, 'I'll get on the radio. We can have a doctor out to take a look at you. You won't be needing any X-ray, but he can check you out and strap you up.'

'This is a damned nuisance for you!' Dan apologised.

Ingo gave his rare, beautiful smile. 'I guess we're both used to every kind of accident in our way of life. I'm only sorry it had to happen and spoil your visit. From our point of view, we're very glad of your company. This spill of yours will give us a chance to enjoy it a bit longer!'

Dan coloured to his ears, stabbed with pleasure. 'Aren't you the guy for diplomacy?'

'He meant it!' Genny said firmly.

'Thank you, Giannina,' Ingo said dryly, 'that saves

93

me repeating myself. I know Flick found all your stories of Texas very thrilling and romantic.'

'It is romantic!' Dan said, his slow drawl swelling with pride.

Genny's dark eyes were sparkling. 'I'd like to see it one day, Dan. All I know is what I've seen in the movies; the Spanish conquistadores, John Wayne and the Indians, the Spanish missions, the great ranches and the oil wells, the desert and the mountains, Mexico across the border, Louisiana, the Gulf. Ingo bought us handbags from that department store in Dallas—I'd like to lose myself there, Austin, Houston, El Paso, San Antonio. Glen Campbell at Galveston!'

'He's waiting there for you!' Dan promised. 'There's nowhere I wouldn't show you. Texas has everything to offer. There's no better place on earth than the Lone Star State, except maybe Tandarro.'

'You're remarkably right!' Genny leaned forward, smiling. 'People usually love their homes best.'

'Feel a sort of traitor if you didn't,' Dan maintained, rubbing his jaw gingerly. 'I don't seem to feel all my teeth!'

'What's a few teeth more or less!' Genny said flippantly.

'Teeth are everything, Miss Genny. I'd sooner break a leg than lose one of my teeth. They're powerful important. I have all my own.'

'Check them now if you're not happy!' she suggested.

'What a pint-sized little pest you are, Giannina!' Ingo put in. 'Poor old Dan's in enough trouble without your teasing him.'

'I swear I don't mind!' Dan grunted with pain. 'In fact, I kinda like it. Don't want to upset Miss Felicity, though. She's a delicate little thing.'

The way he spoke informed them quite clearly that things were developing at a fantastic rate in Dan's mind if nowhere else. Flick the enchantress they were used to, but not every man made his response so immediately plain. For a hardheaded rancher, Dan seemed utterly smitten by the sort of thing Flick had been doing all her life, and it had happened very quickly to a man supposedly terribly shy with women.

When they arrived back at the homestead Flick took over, her lovely face distressed, her blue eyes seeing no one but the injured man; she led him to an armchair, and fussed over him to the extent that no one else appeared to be necessary. Ingo stood there for a few minutes watching Felicity's charming fluttering and Dan's equally touching response, on his dark face an expression of amusement and a faint boredom as though he had seen it all at least a dozen times before. Privately he was marvelling at his cousin's inexhaustible, untroubled capacity for forming relationships. Superficial her feelings might have been, but they were prolific, given over to living out other women's secret dreams. It would have been funny, except that Genny had been affected by her mother's life style. It made him far less inclined to smile.

'If there's nothing else I can do,' he said a little sharply, 'I'd better get back on the job. Spook and the boys are going out on a cattle drive. You can let me know, Flick, if I'm needed. Genny will have got through to the Flying Doctor base by now.'

'Don't worry, darling, I'll look after him!' Felicity promised, keeping her voice capable and soothing. 'Except that you're such a big strong man, Dan, I'd be terribly upset. Really, you've only arrived here. The whole thing's just awful. Take another sip of that brandy now!'

Genny, flying back along the corridor on her way from the radio room, came to a breathless halt at the back of Ingo and grasped his arm.

95

'Well?' He turned his dark head to her, with the inevitable touch of arrogant command.

'Oh!' She just stood there, fighting to transfer her fascinated gaze from her mother and Dan.

'It's all right, Giannina, you're permitted to speak.'

'He's coming, of course. Doctor Murray!' She looked away from Ingo's sparkling, mocking gaze, lifting her voice for Dan's benefit. 'You'll like him, Dan. He's a fine doctor and absolutely one of the funniest men alive. Probably you'll have to put up with a certain amount of ribbing, but it won't kill you.'

'Genny dearest, that will do!' Felicity said with careful firmness, as though Dan had suffered a near-fatal wound.

'All right then, Flick, if you don't need me I'll go with Ingo and annoy him further.'

Felicity's blue eyes looked puzzled, a faint frown on her brow. 'Are you all right, dear, you're acting very strangely!'

'Could I talk to you for a moment, Ingo?' Genny asked, ignoring her mother.

'Perhaps.'

'Can't you do better than that?'

'Not if I want to get any work done. Come on, Giannina, you little monster!'

'Sure you won't be lonely, Dan?' asked Genny.

'Do me a favour, Ingo, and take her away!' Felicity begged.

'If I must. Only her baby curls save her. Sure you'll settle for Flick, Dan? Until the doctor arrives, that is?'

Felicity looked up pointedly at this frontal attack. 'What's got into you two? Honestly, sometimes you both sound the same!'

Dan raised his empty glass in salute. 'Thanks for everything, Ingo, young Genny! I'm not used to a woman fussing over me. Not recently, anyway, not since

Ma died. Miss Felicity reminds me of her in some wonderful way.'

'Hear that, Flick?' Ingo asked dryly.

'Yes, and I'm very glad.'

Ingo put up his hand, a sardonic smile faintly twisting his mouth. 'Well, I'd best get to it. See you later then. We'll spot the Cessna when it comes in. Ask Doc for lunch, Flick, if he's got time. Get Maggie to fix something nice. I'll bring Genny back with me about one-thirty, all right?'

'Right!' Felicity answered briskly, considering her capacity for organisation.

Dan, for a man in pain, looked almost radiant, but before Genny had time to form any comment she was grasped firmly and compelled out into the sunshine. 'Goodness me, Dan's got it bad!' she said when she was able.

'I can only envy him his rosy outlook!' replied Ingo.

'That's a rotten thing to say! What do you mean, anyway?'

'Oh, come on now, kiddo, Flick's going to lead him a fine old parade. What do you think he's going to say when he finds out about Carlo and Stewart and Hughie, not to mention the non-starters?'

'I've already told him,' said Genny simply.

'You've *what*?' He grasped her arm and almost lifted her off the ground.

'You heard.'

'Nice work, cherub! Now why would you do that?'

'Well, you know Flick! She's too modest to speak for herself.'

'I know Flick!' he repeated forcibly. 'Her brain is nearly brand new, she spends so little time using it.'

'You're hurting me, Ingo, and I thought you liked Flick,' she protested.

'Oh, I do! It's her love life I'd like to ignore. Dan is a

97

guest of mine and he's also a client, a good one! I don't want to lose him.'

'Maybe you'll be gaining a cousin-in-law. What's one more anyway? Elizabeth Taylor has been married six times.'

'I don't suppose Flick is trying to beat her record!' Ingo released her abruptly, reaching out a hand and tucking a stray curl back into the shining halo.

'You don't have to thrash out my problems!' Genny said, looking up at him. 'Generally love affairs are very pleasant. What am I worrying about Flick for? She's a grown woman even if no one suspects she's my mother. If she wants to team up with Dan and fly off to Texas, why should I mind?'

'Won't you be getting married yourself?' he asked sardonically.

'The devil I will!'

He raised his eyebrows. 'Why take such fright? What about Dave? You can't experiment round like Flick. I won't let you.'

'I'm afraid for a couple of weeks you'll have to share me with Dave.'

'I'm not that generous!' His hand shot out with devastating speed, turning her towards him. 'What's mine is mine for ever!'

'Heaven knows where you got the idea *I* was your possession!' she protested, sure that in a minute her panic would show.

'I haven't put in all these years for nothing.' He drew her close to him, just holding her. It was breathtaking the amount of feeling he could create in her and she drew in her breath sharply, enkindled by a quick hot rush of desire just to be alone with him, without the need to deny it.

He lifted her head, his silver eyes resting briefly on her face. 'It's a pretty fragile shelter you've built for yourself. Don't count on it to protect you too much longer. Come on, Giannina, we can't stay here talking. I can't cope with you and the station too.'

'You talk down to me all the time!' she said with a strange desperation.

'It won't be for long. You're turning into a woman right in front of my eyes. God knows I've waited long enough for it to happen.'

Blandly he dropped an arm about her slight shoulders, turning her towards the jeep. She said nothing and the two of them moved in perfect rhythm, a mysterious intimacy that had never been there before. Genny had a mad urge to fling her arms about him, crush him if she could, which was ridiculous considering his lean powerful frame.

'Do you think I'm beautiful, Ingo? Do you?'

'Yes, you're beautiful, damn you!'

'Thank you. One of us ought to be friendly. I'm trying.'

He lifted her like a featherweight into the jeep, dropping a hard kiss on her parted mouth. 'Don't try too hard!'

'Why not?' she asked abruptly, touching the tips of her fingers to her burning mouth.

'Don't be so naïve, little one. For all you know I might be madly in love with you.'

'And are you?'

'My God, what a question!'

'I take it the answer is no!'

He gazed at her. 'You could take a man apart if you wanted to!'

'And that's not going to happen to you?'

'My life revolves around Tandarro. What's mine is mine and it will never get away from me.'

'Is that a warning?' Her dark eyes were fixed on his face, her cheeks rather flushed.

'One you can't ignore. You know the score!'

'Talk to me,' she begged him.

'About what?'

'Reality—the way you act like you do. Why you ever bothered to kiss me.'

'That was some occasion. Move over.'

'I keep remembering,' she confessed.

'Naturally.'

'Yet you never tell me anything. I really don't know the first thing about you.'

'Now you want to get me to talk about myself. Giannina darling, you're priceless!'

'I'm only trying to be pleasant.'

'You're breaking my heart!' he mocked.

'I doubt if you've got one.'

'Oh, it's real enough! Who used to pick you up when you cried as a child? It wasn't Flick.'

'You loved me then. Have I really turned into something quite different?'

'Yes,' he said crisply.

'Which leaves me with nothing to say,' Genny concluded.

'And that's a promise?'

'Start the jeep, Ingo,' she said through her clenched teeth. 'If I sit here much longer I'm going to catch fire.'

'Where's your hat?' he asked.

'I don't damned well care!'

'Baby, you have the most beautiful skin. Are you really going to burn it to leather?'

'A lot you'd care!' she snapped.

'On the contrary, I'd make a big fuss!' He reached over to the back seat of the jeep, seeing Genny wasn't moving, retrieved her gaucho hat and rammed it on her silky curls. They rayed out like silver whorls against the black brim, making the most enchanting frame for her face.

'Well?' she said rather aggressively, returning his frank stare.

'Yes, well, I might feel like heading off to where no one would ever find us, but I'm not going to do it!'

'Good for you, because I wouldn't go along with it.'

'So you say!' he said mockingly. 'Why can't you be a woman instead of a perverse child?'

'Tandarro is all that keeps you going,' she retorted.

'You want to be supported, don't you?'

He had spoken carelessly as he put the jeep in motion and reversed it out of the shade, his dark profile relaxed, yet she swung her head towards him with a kind of urgency.

'You don't support us, Ingo. Or do you?'

'Why would it annoy you?'

'You know perfectly well I'd be prepared to get a job if that was so!'

'Mind telling me why?'

'You don't, do you?'

'I don't, as you say. Flick has her own money, and occasionally I give her a little something. That's quite common knowledge and none of your business. Flick happens to be one of my great favourites despite herself.'

'I really would care!' exclaimed Genny.

'How terrible!' he said as though he didn't care at all. 'That's rather pathetic, the idea of your working.'

'I could do it.'

'So you keep telling me. But seeing you're such a clever girl we'll have to insist on you finishing your education. A doctor's wife is expected to turn herself into something!'

'You have an infinite capacity for riling me!'

'Did you say *ruling*?'

'That too. It puts me on the defensive.'

'A salutary experience for one too accustomed to getting her own way. Tell me, have you thought out anything to keep Dave entertained?'

'Nothing in particular. We should have a house full —Trish and the kids, and darling Sally for sure. I bet you've thought out your plans there. Dan looks like staying on with Flick all set to show him a good time. A full house!'

'The only kind to have. Even Evvy asked me could she invite old Lady Maxwell.'

'That's too full!' Genny said, surprised.

'She mightn't come, with the whole State her oyster. Still, Evvy did ask me, which is more than I can say for you.'

Genny looked eager. 'What about giving a big wonderful gala party and inviting everybody? We could open up the ballroom. It's so beautiful and it's never used!'

'All my fault! My way of life hasn't permitted dancing up to date. God knows why it was ever built. There must have been lunacy in the family.'

'And it hasn't burned itself out!'

Ingo grinned. 'You can say that again! Flick will probably want to announce her engagement.'

'If I thought that, I'd break down and cry.'

'Better if you don't. I might have to stop and comfort you.'

She sat up straight and smiled at him, her heart, had she known it, right in her eyes. 'That settles it! Nothing would make me fall into your arms again.'

'I think you will.'

His answering smile tore at her senses. Pure devastation, impeccable white teeth in a dark, self-contained face. 'Smile at me like that,' she said slowly, 'and I'll fall in love with you.'

'Nothing would surprise me. A girl like you lights her own fires.'

'And it isn't safe!' she wailed.

'You seem to be enjoying yourself.'

'I'm in search of myself.'

'I know it.'

'You know me too well.'

'Perhaps—Genny, the little girl. It's Giannina, the woman, I have to reach.'

She shivered at the caressing note in his voice and fell silent. She needed time to consider all the reckless overwhelming emotions he was arousing in her that she couldn't quite control since he had held her in his arms and shown her the force of her own feelings, nothing could ever be the same again. Her reaction to him, passionate and headlong, had flowed naturally, when for years now she had hardly been able to talk to him without flying into a fury. Ingo had not been notably kind and patient with her either. Flick had even assumed they were incompatible except for the odd times when the storms had broken and they achieved the perfect rapport that had been normal in her childhood. Ingo's influence on her had been remarkable. She had always wanted and needed his company even when she had cried out unabashed and unrepentant that she hated him, like there was no other way. Ingo the known and the unknown. Ingo, Big Brother. Ingo, a lover. The thought suddenly frightened her, making the blood surge through her veins. Unconsciously her expression had become tense, a small pulse throbbing at the base of her throat, colour staining her cheekbones, darkening her velvety brown eyes to black.

Ingo glanced at her, reading her mind with no difficulty. She had taken a very long time to arrive at that possibility and her young panic was showing. His eyes slipped over her slender body and his hard, handsome mouth softened. No one could be sweeter than Genny when she was frightened.

'Don't lose your cool, baby!' he said lightly.

She lifted her head, her expression very soft. 'I'm like that with you.'

'You're very temperamental, I have to admit. You're also shatteringly beautiful!'

'Am I?' she asked, honestly unaware of her own sexuality.

'Don't let's talk about it!' Ingo groaned, his silver-grey eyes very cool and full of self-mockery.

'And that's what's wrong with everyone!' she protested, her quick temper stirring. 'No communication!'

'We can communicate, stupid!'

'No, we can't!'

'Let's test that out!'

She stared at him, but he seemed completely serious, pulling the jeep off the track and running it in under a glossy-leafed tree. He switched off the ignition and turned to her, his light eyes sparkling in contrast to his darkly tanned skin, 'You were talking about communication.'

'Oh, really!' she started to say, her heart thumping.

'I do believe you're nervous,' he drawled.

'Do you think I'm fool enough to ask for a repeat performance?' she demanded.

'I'll bet you ten to one you are!'

'You'd better apologise!' she threatened.

'It would take a big, big man to do that!' he taunted.

'Isn't that what you are? I mean, I've had years and years of personal attention with a kind word now and then!'

'Then why call me Black Ingo?'

'I didn't know just how *right* I was. Now I really believe it. Black Ingo!'

'You picked the wrong time, baby!'

'You said you'd take care of me!'

'Well, this is what happens!' He reached for her,

ignoring her cry if he even heard it, his hands clamped high around her narrow rib cage, hard and taut.

'Don't use me for target practice!' she cried feverishly, acutely sensitive to his frightening strength. 'Just because Sally's not around.'

'Who's Sally?' he asked.

'Do you *have* to?' she clenched her fists and hit at him. 'Oh, listen, Ingo, you scare me!'

It was true, because excitement was leaping jaggedly right through her like a lick of flame, going higher and higher and threatening to devour her like a fire out of control. It was almost unbearable, and her enormous doe eyes began to drown in tears.

He released her abruptly, the dangerous deliberation going out of his face. 'I see what you mean,' he said in a low, even voice. 'Relax, cherub, you're in no danger. That alarm in your eyes is one hundred per cent genuine. It even upsets me.'

Shaken, she slid down into the seat again, half collapsing against his shoulder. 'I never thought that after all these years ... I mean, it's impossible! I can't think what it's all about.'

'You love me and we both know it!'

She tilted her head back, staring at him. '*No*. No, I don't!'

'What is it you feel?'

'Just a tremendous response. You make me come alive—too alive. It's breathless, like a disaster. Ravishing, like crossing over into the desert and losing your bearings. Nothing's the same again. But that's *me*, just a child so far as I can see. You're way ahead of me, terribly sure of yourself, ready for anything. It could be a new game for you. You've trained yourself for years and years now to an iron control—turn it on, turn it off. You don't really need anyone.'

'Don't say any more!' he said with icy disfavour.

'It isn't possible I've hurt you?'

He put a hard finger along her cheek, turning her face towards him. 'Would I let you, you silly little girl?'

'How long are we going to go on like this?' she sighed.

'Does it matter all that much?'

He sounded unbearably cynical and she moved very carefully right up against him, laying her lips along his cheek. 'Now listen, Ingo, don't sound like that. You worry me.'

'Stop it! You could have made a great actress. How does your Dave kiss you?'

'Oh, something like this!' she murmured, kissing him very quietly on the corner of his mouth. 'Agreeable. Controllable. A warm glow, you know!' She didn't say that her pleasure at that moment was glaring. 'Now *you*, you outpace me in every way. It's like a fight for survival. A takeover with kisses for bribes!'

'How graphic,' he said sardonically.

'If I let you, you could bring me to breaking point!'

'Poor little Giannina! What a nightmare! Ravished by her wicked cousin.'

'That's one way of looking at it,' she said coolly. 'Also you're a good deal older than I am and I'd never catch up with you either!'

The flash in his eyes was part amusement. 'And what am I supposed to say? *Ciao*, baby, see you some time? I didn't know we were locked in some kind of sexist duel.'

'What makes you think you've got to be the boss?' she challenged him.

'Because I'm one of the lucky ones. It's the way I'm made. Do you particularly want to be treated like a little man? The trouble with you is that you want it all ways. Women are the real dictators. Haven't you seen Maggie pushing Ted around? Half his size, too. She won't even leave him with a mumbling word.'

'She's a terrific cook!' Genny pointed out fairly. 'It's only Ted she snaps at. I think he even likes it.'

'God forbid! That kind of thing would be impossible to tolerate.'

She slid her hat off her head and settled herself gently into his somehow accommodating shoulder. 'It's moments like these when I can't help feeling I'm complaining about nothing!'

'Don't I know it!' he rejoined.

'One of our perfect moments again,' she said with an ecstatic sigh. 'It's like a fantasy. Our other world turned upside down!' With something like elation she twined her fingers through his, not anticipating the betraying urgency that drove her to rain a series of featherlight kisses along his hard jawline. She heard her own voice, very soft and shaken, almost endeavouring to explain her own spontaneous actions. 'It's a paradox, I know, but you're physically perfect to me. In fact you're really a very beautiful man.'

His low laugh was sharp and derisive. 'Do you mind? A man's not beautiful.'

'A differing order of beauty, but beauty all the same,' she affirmed.

'Then what are you so frightened about anyway?'

'Oh, I don't know!' she said, half mesmerised by the feel of his hand in her hair. 'Whatever it was, I've forgotten. Right now I'd do anything to make you happy!'

'Then I'm going to take what I want at this moment!'

He lifted her shining head to him, his hand sliding down to shape her creamy nape, a curious expression very like tenderness on his handsome dark face. She could only look back at him, knowing what he was going to do, but affected by the same drug, a fevered sensual awareness that sprang up between them, linking them with a delicate violence; a demand as exquisite as it was terrible. Her mouth parted instinctively, accepting him before he even touched her. In spite of everything she was going to allow this torrent of emotion to engulf her. She lifted her hand almost in a trance to bring his head down to her in the last moment, clinging to him, lifting her slender arms and locking them about his neck. If this was possession it was inescapable. Ingo's hold on her could never be broken. She experienced one moment of resistance, then she let it all close over her like a dark golden storm. A man as complex, as compelling as Ingo was bound to consider her his private property, over-indulged in one way, but a possession without question. She was saying his name over and over against his mouth, her heart beating in agitation, wildly disturbed. All his tremendous energy and authority, all she had ever resented, now held all the magic in the world. Her body gave a half agonised shudder as though her feelings were too strong for her.

'Genny?'

She lay back against him, her dark eyes wide open, full of the urgency that fired her blood. 'I need you so desperately. You're rather cruel!'

'If I am I'm being cruel to both of us!'

'I'd like to fly straight off into the sun!' she said on a wave of reaction.

'I'll fix anything for you, but not that!' he murmured.

'Your name *is* Ingo, isn't it?'

'And what do you know about me?'

'I'm learning fast.'

'That's what you're here for!'

'Is the world swinging around or are we?' she inquired.

'You're rambling, darling!' he said, tumbling her soft curls.

'Damn, there you go again. I'm the idiot and you're the devilish adult.'

'There are times one just has to let the fires fizzle out. I'm dead set on abiding by a ruthless set of rules. You're my sweet little Genny, and you're an innocent for all your incomparable allure.'

'It seems to me now you've coloured my thoughts for all the days of my life,' she said softly.

'Well, let's say you've come through the worst of your adolescence.'

She tried to sit up, failed the first time and allowed him to help her. 'I won't risk any more comments. What do we do now?'

'I thought you'd never ask. I want to ride out with Spook and the rest for part of the way. You can come!'

'What a delightful invitation! Thank you.'

'Put your hat on!'

'Yes, boss!' she said in an excellent imitation of Spook's melancholy voice which actually earned him his nickname. He glanced back at her with some amusement, his silver-grey eyes gleaming, noting and accepting the subtle radiance that lay over her, heightening her beauty. Already they had come out of yesterday.

)

CHAPTER FIVE

THE feeling of discovery and mutual attraction persisted for Felicity and Dan in the week that followed. If there was nothing strange in that from Felicity's point of view, it was an original, authentic love affair for Dan. According to plan he should have been on his way home to Texas, instead of which he was thoroughly enjoying the Australian Outback with every last comfort and the company of a very beautiful woman. It was simply a miracle since he expected to die a bachelor. The breaking of a collar-bone was not the minor disaster it had at first seemed; in fact Dan now looked on it as heavenly intervention, very likely at his mother's instigation. She had always been a good scheming woman in life.

The terrible thought of Felicity's three husbands Dan pushed right to the back of his mind, submerged but not forgotten. In short, he was properly caught up in the web of Felicity's fascination, temporarily blind to her case history. The truly extraordinary part was that Felicity appeared to him, as she did to most everyone else, as an innocent, ravishingly pretty little woman who had been unfortunate enough to have her life tied up to at least two drop-outs. In that evaluation, Dan was as ignorant of the true facts as everyone else, with the exclusion of Felicity's family, for Felicity was a queen bee by nature, irresistibly trapping the male and demanding unswerving allegiance.

If things seemed perfect for Felicity and Dan, Genny was worried and Aunt Evelyn was caustic in their private conversation. Ingo, of course, refused to take any responsibility in the matter, though his sympathies were with Dan. With the expected arrival of a house full of guests, Genny finally came to the conclusion that she had best have it out with her mother. Felicity was notoriously capricious, but it was as plain as an approaching dust storm that Dan was as desperately in love as any young man. If Felicity failed him, Genny considered it very likely that Dan would attempt to ride the piebald again, with the inevitable results. If she was really interfering it was from the very best motives. After years of experience she never hesitated to act for the best.

Felicity, when Genny sought her out that evening

before dinner, was busy in her room, brushing out her lovely hair, totally involved in the operation. When she caught sight of her daughter in the open doorway, she turned away from the triple-mirrored dressing table to smile.

'Come in, darling, but do shut the door in case Evvy goes by. I really think my hair suits me better this way, don't you? Short hair is always nicer for the summer.'

'You look gorgeous, Flick, any way.' Genny shut the door carefully and walked into the huge bedroom. It was her favourite, but Flick always beat her to it. She pulled around a Louis XVII armchair covered in silk brocade and sank into it, with her back to the marble mantel and the tall antique mirror in its elaborate gilded frame.

Felicity was talking in her soft appealing voice as she flicked up the curls on her nape. 'What do you think I should wear tonight? A stupid shame, what happened to the green.'

'I've never been known to give Melly anything to iron,' answered Genny.

'Well, I didn't think she'd put a hole through it. She's such a sweet little thing.'

'Actually that's not her job, Flick. She helps Maggie in the kitchen, as you very well know. Dropping things is more in Melly's line. Any dinner service is lucky to survive. Anyway, I wanted to talk to you about something else.'

'No doubt it's Dave?' said Felicity, making provocative eyes.

'There are others I'll start on first. What about the Lone Ranger?'

'Now there's a charming man! And that fascinating drawl. I could listen to it for ever, it's so musical!'

'Wonderful, my faith is restored.'

The slight asperity in Genny's voice brought Felicity

111

around on her stool. 'What are you talking about, darling? Really, all that education has only made you that wee bit difficult to understand.'

'Then I'll spell it out in big letters. Dan's in love with you, Flick.'

Felicity gave her enigmatic little smile and picked up the brush again.

'Don't smirk, Flick. It's serious.'

'It will do him good!' Felicity maintained imperturbably.

'I suppose so. The only hitch is that eventually I feel sure he's going to ask you to marry him,' her daughter told her.

'And that's all right too!'

'You mean you *would* marry him?'

'I confess I've given it some thought.'

'Serious thought?' pressed Genny.

'Surely you don't think anything else?'

'You don't love him, Flick!' Genny said quietly.

Felicity paused. 'What's love? Tell me, chicken, what is it?'

'It's the biggest challenge there is.'

'Exactly.'

'I'm sure we don't mean it in the same way.'

Felicity found her daughter's eyes in the mirror. 'Don't spoil such a lovely evening, darling. You're so intense about everything. Honestly, sometimes I have to shut my eyes in case I see Carlo sitting there beside you.'

'That's nice! Would you mind not knocking my father so much?'

'But I loved him!' Felicity protested, opening her eyes wide. 'You're not spoiling for a fight, are you, Genny? You know how I suffer from headaches. Honestly, it's a fight all the way when you get in these deep moods.' Felicity rose to her feet and stood on the tips

112

of her toes, her body in the lace and chiffon robe as slender and graceful as a young girl's. 'Dan has a lot of money,' she said at last, thoughtfully.

'Is that part of it?' Genny asked, dismayed.

'Yep!' Felicity whooped, expecting Genny to laugh, but she didn't, her dark eyes very serious.

'But surely, Flick, we're comfortably off. I mean, we can only have so much of everything. Do you really need any more? It doesn't seem decent.'

'The truth is, darling, I'm not the least bit decent about money. I never have been. Besides, I want money of my own.'

There was an instant of shocked comprehension before Genny came to her feet, taking a few steps towards her mother, who fell back against the bedpost. 'Really, you do remind me most unsuitably of your father! The only man to strike me. Just you stay where you are, my girl. I've never told you before—now you know. I've been absolutely broke in between marriages, by our standards, that is.'

'I don't believe it!' Genny murmured, feeling suddenly empty. 'Everyone thinks we have money.'

'It's just part of the game. Keeping up appearances. It's Faulkner money, Gen. Ingo is the big wheeler-dealer. Surely you realise that?'

'If it's true I'll die of shame.'

'You will *not* die!' Felicity insisted, scrutinising her daughter closely. 'Why shouldn't Ingo support us? He has tons of money, you wouldn't believe it. I'm surprised you're the least bit concerned.'

'But what about Hughie?' Genny asked intently.

'Hughie was a dear man but a big disappointment. Death duties took most of it; what was left wasn't nearly enough. Why, it scarcely bought me a couple of really good dresses.'

Genny winced. 'You pay far **too** much for your

clothes, Flick, I've always told you that. I suppose Ingo has been paying my fees as well?'

'Certainly. I haven't. I don't know that I'm altogether in favour of higher education for young girls. It makes them dissatisfied. Don't worry about Ingo, I'm sure it makes him feel good.'

'It doesn't make *me* feel good!' Genny said rather bitterly.

'Oh, you're a regular little volcano, ready to go off at a moment's notice,' mocked Felicity. 'What's the big deal, darling? It's Ingo's duty to throw a little money in our direction. He's my cousin and he has all of this. It's unreasonable to keep it all to himself. We're just two frail little creatures.'

'I'm glad there aren't any more of us!' Genny said soberly. 'You can't marry Dan for security, Flick. Apart from anything else, you must respect the depth of his feeling for you. Don't sell him short.'

'And don't you tell me how to keep a man happy. After all ...'

'When you tire of them, Flick,' Genny broke in on her, 'you just throw them out the window, but you'll never get rid of Dan that way. He's too big and he's not as easy-going as he makes out. There's iron under that gentle manner. Don't shut your eyes to reality. The woman who married Dan would have to toe the line, not gather rosebuds along the way.'

'Well, if you *must* know,' Felicity said with a hand to her breast, 'it's not only security, though in my opinion that's a good enough reason at my age.'

'I've never heard you mention your age before!' Genny said in surprise.

'Well, I may look a dozen years younger than I am, but I don't know at precisely what time in the future I might suddenly crumple. I've lived on my looks all my life and I've been loved for them, but Dan is the kind of man who would still love me when I started going to pieces.'

'It's equally true that he wants and expects a square deal,' Genny said.

'Really, darling, there's no need to point that out. You and Ingo both treat me as if I'm brainless and poor old Evvy looks right through me, the brittle old maid.'

'Then forgive us, Flick. I was only worried that you might be amusing yourself at Dan's expense.'

'So I am!' Felicity laughed enchantingly, running a caressing hand down over her slim hips. 'And why shouldn't I? Life is a wonderful game, Genny. You're so wretchedly *earnest*!'

'I could wish you were the same! If you married Dan, and we're somehow assuming he's going to ask you, you'd be living on the other side of the world.'

'So what's the big drama? Americans are just as civilised as we are. I've seen you enjoying Dan's company.'

'Well, I like him. We all do. He's a fine man,' Genny smiled, 'intelligent and humorous and tolerant.'

'Well then?'

'He's not being too calm and sensible about you. I'd miss you terribly, Flick.'

'But darling,' Felicity threw up her hands, 'you would be coming with us. I know Dan would just love to have you. Why, you're so pretty you could get into movies.'

'I'd say that was a career to be scrupulously avoided,' Genny said wryly. 'This is my country, Flick. I'm an Australian.'

'Your father was an Italian,' Felicity said reasonably.

'No matter, I've made my throw and it's all for Australia. I've got great faith in my own country. It's a slumbering giant at the moment. I want to be around when it wakes up. I love it!'

'So do I!' Felicity protested, a little embarrassed by all this patriotism.

'Then I take it you're serious about Dan?'

'I never said *that*, exactly.'

'Don't hurt him, Flick!' implored Genny. 'He's such a nice man.'

'And he's big enough to take care of himself!' Felicity returned somewhat tartly.

'He should be, but don't be surprised if he reacts a little foolishly. Have you told him about your previous weddings?'

'That's for me to decide. thank you, my darling.'

'You mean you haven't told him yet?' demanded Genny.

'Should I have?'

'If you're going to give him an even chance, *yes*!'

Felicity walked with her light graceful step back to the dressing-table, picking up her brush, examining it closely. 'Dan's gone beyond the point of caring about anything like that. Eventually I'll tell him. I'm sure he'll understand I've been very unlucky to have had my life strewn with so many failures.'

'And you'd like another turn?' Genny asked flatly.

Her mother stiffened. 'Surely that's my business? Shouldn't you keep out of it, pet?'

'I'm in to the death, Flick. You see, I love you and we've gone through a lot together. Why did you never tell me that Ingo was taking care of us?'

'That was part of the deal!' Felicity said, looking down at her polished toenails. 'Ingo wanted it that way and I'd advise you not to tell him you know any different. Really, Genny, for an intelligent girl you've taken a long time to come to it. You know I fling money around like confetti.'

'On purpose. The fact it's not really ours doesn't seem to bother you,' Genny said bitterly.

'Why should it? Ingo is my cousin and my dearest friend. He loves me in a very pure kind of way. He loves you too, though not quite as much. Come to that, he was fonder of you as a child than of his own sister. I know Trish used to get nearly hysterical about it in her younger days. Thank God she's settled down—marriage did that for her. It will be nice to have her here, and the children. I love the little boy. Why, it's not even too late to have one of my own!'

Genny knocked an ornament off the side table and bent to retrieve it, mercifully unbroken. 'You're joking!' she managed in a hollow kind of voice.

'Of course I'd need a husband!' Felicity said gaily. 'It's not uncommon for a woman my age to have another baby, you know.'

Genny laughed. 'Flick, you never cease to surprise me. In fact, I'm struck speechless!'

'I'm somewhat surprised myself. It's a long time since I've been anywhere near a nursery.'

'If you're thinking along those lines, are you sure you don't love Dan?'

'I think he's a wonderful man. I might surprise him and give him a son!'

'Good God, there's a challenge!'

'A pity there's not another method,' Felicity mused. 'I'd hate to spoil my figure, but it would only be temporary. I eat like a bird, as you know.'

'No, I didn't know. I thought you had a fairly hearty appetite myself!' Genny turned her head aside, uncertain whether to laugh or to cry. Somewhere deep inside her she was hurting badly, she couldn't think exactly why. 'Well, Flick, I'd better dress for dinner.'

'Wear that yellow dress I bought you. It's one of your best colours. I don't like to keep harping on Texas, but isn't there some song about a yellow rose?'

'Bless your little heart, there is!' Genny said, getting to her feet and turning the chair to face the fireplace.

'Get Dan to sing it to you while you're holding hands out there on the veranda.'

'I know, darling, you're lonely. Think how nice it will be to have Dave here. By the way, Ingo's picking Trish and the kids up. He's taking you.'

'He never said a word about it to me,' said Genny, startled.

'Well, you know Ingo!' Felicity smiled. 'Everyone falls in with his arrangements.'

'It must be a family trait,' was the response.

'Naughty, darling!'

'I'm beginning to feel like a mere pawn.'

'Now, now, you're my darling daughter. Really you'd love it in Texas.'

'Better wait until you're asked, Flick.'

'Hasn't anyone ever told you *I* do the asking?'

'Take a tip from your daughter,' said Genny. 'Let Dan do it his way. He's used to playing the big, strong man!'

Felicity spun round, looking happy. 'You didn't tell me what to wear. Something cool and easy—what about the halter-neck?'

'Dan has enough to cope with as it is. It must be frustrating for him not to run off with you now,' Genny said dryly.

Felicity suddenly saw her daughter. 'You sound edgy, darling. It's missing Dave, that's what it is.'

'Would it do me any good to disagree?' Genny said a shade wearily. 'Wear the halter-neck, Flick. Dan will think it's terrific.'

'We could be sisters!' Felicity cried, living only to be loved and admired.

'That's how I think of you, Flick, a younger sister. I never wanted a mother. They're not strictly necessary.'

Outside in the hallway, Genny dashed the tears from

her eyes. She was becoming over-emotional these days. Her head down, she careered into Ingo, who brought her to attention, meeting her eyes squarely.

'What's up?'

The question was terse but concerned. Genny didn't answer him, caught up in the miasma of inexplicable sadness. Her shoulders were drooping and her vital young face looked slightly martyred. It appeared to irritate him, for he half dragged her off towards his study, shutting the door.

'I said what's up?'

'Not a damn thing!'

'I can hardly bear the way you swear. You've come out of Flick's room and you're crying.'

'I haven't got a single friend,' she burst out.

'*Genny!*' He pushed her gently down on to the sofa. 'I'm here. You're not hopelessly adrift in the cruel, cruel world, you know.'

'Why didn't you tell me?' she said, her shoulders lifting in a heartfelt sigh.

'About what?' He made a funny little sound of exasperation, bending forward and tipping her face up.

'You're the Godfather!'

He smiled at her, but his silver-grey eyes were hard and steely. 'So Flick told you?'

'She didn't tell me exactly. It just slipped out.'

'How does it feel?'

'Terrible,' she confessed.

He threw up his arrogant dark head. 'Did you really think I was going to let you battle on your own?'

'You should have told me, Ingo. I had a right to know.'

'What I want to know is why Flick should tell you *now*,' he said grimly.

'Flick is thinking of flying off to Texas,' Genny said

abruptly, something inside her boiling over in mute rage.

Ingo didn't appear to take it too seriously. 'Flick likes to daydream,' he said calmly.

'I think she's serious.'

'Poor old Dan!'

'There's nothing wrong with Flick!' she said with only a shadow of her usual spirit.

'Want a few examples of her scatty ways?' he inquired.

She bristled. 'I thought you were trying to pacify me.'

'Oh, I am. Why are you crying?'

'It must be my age. Maybe I'm going neurotic.'

'I think Flick has worn you down. If she wants to go to Texas, we'll sure as hell let her!'

'She expects *me* to go.'

'Oh no!' he said emphatically. 'You're staying here. I can't even think of holidays at the moment. Flick had better understand that.'

'It's a good thing I'm through my finals, or I will be. I worked well all year.'

'Oh, what's going to happen now?' he inquired sardonically, leaning back against the desk.

'I'll get a job, of course.'

Ingo nodded. 'Most people have them. It's about time you justified your existence. What about Dave?'

'Don't talk about Dave!' she said a little wildly, expecting him to have taken a different line. 'I don't want to talk about Dave.'

'You invited him here,' he pointed out reasonably. 'He'll arrive in a few days.'

'Oh, don't, Ingo!' she said forlornly. 'I'm in dangerously low spirits. You want to hear something else? Flick is thinking of having another child!'

For a minute he towered above her, then he put a hand on her shoulder. 'Help me to sit down.'

'It could even be dangerous!'

'God!' he gave a soft laugh and put his arm about her shoulder. 'One of the things I admire about Flick is her ability to stun you. Is she going mad? A cat would make a better mother.'

'Oh, don't destroy everything!' she wailed, half blinded by tears.

'Why in God's name are you crying?' he asked sharply, at the same time chaining her small frame to him. 'This sort of thing happens regularly with Flick. Oh, stop that, Gen. I can't stand it!'

'I'm just as upset about you!' she continued.

'Damn it, baby, I'm your friend. You believed it when you were small, why not now?' She was sniffing delicately and he whipped out a clean handkerchief. 'I'm afraid this little cry was way overdue. If there's anything else important to say, say it now.'

'There's not a single person I prefer to you,' she gulped.

'What a blesing! Listen, Giannina, Flick loves you dearly, but in her own way. No one and nothing really captures her attention outside of herself.'

'I hope no one says that of me.'

He shook his head. 'You're as different from Flick as you could be and you've carried the burden of her long enough. If Dan wants to take her on, let him.'

'Flick is my *mother*!' she said, starting to cry again. 'My mother, Ingo, don't you understand that? I don't want her to make any more mistakes.'

He lifted her small mournful face, her dark eyes drowned in tears. 'Haven't you noticed she's emerged from them relatively unscathed? You're the one with the scars. Flick's fragility is false. She's really very good at taking punishment and brilliant at dishing it out. She's come through things that would have driven you frantic. Don't look like that, Genny, your face is as desolate as a small child's. I've never tasted the flavour of your tears—you'll move me to do it in a moment and I mightn't be able to stop.'

She was searching for something unfathomable in his face. 'What would happen if we were ever really all alone?'

'Nothing you would ever regret. There's nothing strange or disturbing about me.'

'But you're *both*!' she said wildly. 'And so familiar as well. I can't explain it. When you touch me it's like standing in a blinding ray of light. I can't see anything, all I can do is feel. It's something I've never known before and it's a little frightening. Everything about you draws me to you like a butterfly rushing into the lantana. It's odd!' She dropped her head on to his shoulder and left it there, quite spent.

He didn't speak for a minute, then she heard his dark attractive voice. 'Are you O.K. there?'

Genny nodded. 'Sure. It's absurd how I cling to you. I mean, it's a long way from all the fights we've had!'

'They were good too. I've been thinking, who said Flick was making a mistake? Dan is a fine man. There's even a chance he could make Flick behave.'

'It seems to me that none of them have been able to do that,' she returned.

'Wouldn't you say Dan was an improvement on them all? Flick isn't as young as she used to be. I think she's just about ready to settle down, but naturally if she decides to make a break, that won't include you.'

'I'd best get used to being on my own,' Genny said.

'You're almost totally mine,' murmured Ingo, then: 'I'm picking Trish and the kids up tomorrow. Want to come?'

'Won't you manage all right without me?'

'I'll ignore that. Trish likes you and the kids are your friends. Besides, I want your company.'

'I don't suppose I'll ever be able to pay you back,' she sighed.

'For what?'

She shrugged. 'For making life bearable for God knows how long. For what you've done for Flick.'

'Not Flick. *You*. I did it all for you.'

'Me?' she said, lifting her head.

'I can't tell a lie. I'd have helped Flick out, of course, but you were the one that needed protection, some semblance of a family!'

'Well done, Ingo Faulkner!' she said, rubbing her cheek against his shirt. 'I should feel happier about it.'

'You've got a melancholy streak, and oh, what it does to me! Get up, cherub. We both have to change for dinner.'

'What time shall we leave in the morning?' she asked.

'Nine or a bit after. Trish could have made it here on her own, but I don't want her to go to all that trouble. The kids will enjoy coming in on our own plane.'

'Trish used to be jealous of me once.'

Ingo nodded. 'I know.'

'Nothing's simple, is it?'

'Trish was displaced as a child; I think she's made out very well considering. Ian and the kids have helped a lot.'

'But your mother, no,' she mused.

'I don't want to talk about my mother, Genny.' He looked down at her with hard, gleaming eyes.

'That's sad. She was torn up too, you know.'

'Yes, she was very unhappy, I believe.'

'She couldn't have wanted to ...'

'Leave me?' He drew a short hostile breath, his white teeth snapping. 'She couldn't have been very attached to me, either.'

'Your father was a very powerful man. She couldn't have gone against him.'

'Would you leave your son?' His silver eyes seemed to stab her. 'No, Genny, you wouldn't. I *know* you. My mother left me, now I'm content never to see her again.'

'She couldn't fail to be aware of that, yet Trish sees her all the time.'

'Certainly. What Trish does is entirely her own business, but I'm not going to expend any time or sympathy on my mother. She's been provided for more than adequately, but there will never be any polite invitations from me. She'll never set foot on Tandarro again.'

'You mean it, don't you?'

He looked at her reprovingly, a hard, very formidable man, his glittery eyes narrowed. 'Yes, I do!'

'But she's suffered all these years, Ingo!'

'A familiar argument, and one that doesn't move me.'

'She never remarried,' Genny pointed out.

'Sound thinking on her part. I would never have given her a penny if she had.'

'You're not your father, Ingo!' she said a little desperately. 'He left your mother nothing, but you're a much more compassionate man, bigger in every way. Can't you be more generous now?'

'No, I can't, and it would be a whole lot safer for you to get off the subject. Feeling better?'

She sighed. 'How do I look?'

'The same way you've looked since you were a child. I'm beginning to ask myself if I've ever seen anyone else *but* you.'

'Well, I've always been your usual target. I know deep down that Trish still resents me.'

'The repercussions of an unhappy childhood are endless,' observed Ingo. 'Trish is making a success of her marriage. It's giving her confidence.'

'But she never had you!'

'Oh, shut up,' he said briskly, 'just be thankful you did!'

The trip to Adelaide, instead of being the usual pleasant jaunt, turned into a nightmare with no warning. The flight in had been smooth and uneventful, with a hire car waiting for them at the airport to take them out to the charming leafy-garden suburb where Ian and Trish lived. It was a beautiful day, sparkling and sunny, and Genny particularly liked Adelaide; a very graceful, prosperous city with more tranquillity than most. Ingo, too, was in an unusually relaxed mood which made his pitchfork into white-hot anger all the more unbearable.

When they pulled into Trish's drive there was no sign of the children, which in itself was remarkable, for they could never see enough of their uncle, not to speak of the proposed ride in his speedy, luxurious six-seater to his fabulous property. Genny had been rather expecting acrobats on the lawn, instead of which perfect peace prevailed: flowers blooming, bees humming, birds singing, someone mowing a lawn up there beyond the trees, the slow lazy days of summer.

'Sure we're at the right house?' she said, smiling.

'It's not the same as usual, I grant you. Where do you suppose the kids are? I've got these things I promised them.'

'I'll go in and round them up,' offered Genny.

'Tell Trish I'd like a good strong cup of coffee.'

'Women usually think of these things.'

'Just remind her. She tends to sit around talking.'

'Damn it, she's got to say hello! Why can't a man be more reasonable?'

'Why can't a woman just give in and do what she's told?' he demanded.

'Right, boss!' She walked away jauntily, while Ingo

climbed out of the car and went to the boot where he had stored a box full of fascinating junk that the children had been uncommonly drawn to on their last visit. Genny knocked on the front door and stood back a little, admiring all the flowering plants. A second later Trish came to the door, opening it wide in welcome, but fluttering almost nervously, her grey eyes as soft as a dove's and completely lacking the silvery sparkle that made Ingo's eyes so striking. Still, she resembled her brother, which made her an exceptionally good-looking young woman, but without Ingo's inbred attractive arrogance that could on occasions amount to a frightening formidability. Trish was almost diffident and she was definitely unsettled.

Genny leaned forward curiously, grasping her hand. 'Surely we've got the right day? Anything wrong, Trish?'

'No, no, of course not. Come in, Gen. You look terrific as always. You make me feel like a dull old housewife.'

'That's weird talk! It must be very pleasant to be a dull old housewife with her own lovely home and her husband and children. Where are the kids? I can't wait to see them!'

'They're upstairs,' answered Trish.

'Gosh, have you got them tied up?'

'They'll be down in a little while.'

'Good. Ingo will be here soon—he's got a box of tricks for them, the one they made such a big fuss about last time.'

'I don't remember,' Trish said vaguely.

'I do,' grinned Genny. 'I had to sit down with them and count all the pieces of opal matrix.'

As she was speaking she was wandering into the elegant, contemporary living room. She saw nothing at first, coming in from the strong sunlight; then she saw a woman seated in an armchair, her dark head held erect, almost regal. Genny wasn't prepared for any such confrontation and the shock was tearing, almost robbing her of her voice.

'Mrs Faulkner!' she said, in an upset whisper.

The woman smiled and got up, moving slowly towards Genny, most definitely Ingo's mother. 'It has to be Genny!' she said gravely, in a low, cultured voice. 'How beautiful you are, dear. Your photographs don't do you justice with such rare colouring!'

Genny was responding automatically, taking the extended hand, thin and long fingered and visibly trembling. 'Ingo is here with me,' she said painfully.

'Yes.' Marianne Faulkner looked past her with the strangest expression, almost mystic and imponderably sad.

'He hasn't changed, Mrs Faulkner.'

'I know what you're trying to tell me, child.'

Genny swallowed. 'Should you expose yourself to more pain?'

'I'll never have enough time to beg his forgiveness!'

'Please, Mrs Faulkner!' Genny said, desperate to protect her from what must surely come.

'Don't worry, don't worry. I trust you, Genny. You have very loving eyes. Life hasn't been easy for you either. I can see traces of Felicity in you—the nose and the cheekbones, the petite figure. Flick's hair was never your colour, I think, more silver than gold. How is she?'

'She's well and happy, Mrs Faulkner. I'll tell her you were asking about her.'

'Do that, my dear. I always liked her.' The conversation was well meant, sincere, but a valiant attempt to act normally. There were fine tremors running through those long fingers.

'I feel as though I'm going to faint,' said Trish, deliberately looking down at the floor. 'Ingo's going to resent this deeply.'

'It was my idea. I wanted it,' Marianne Faulkner said with great quietness. 'I wanted to see my son.'

'You're going to!' Genny said with equal intensity, and gripped that frail hand.

From the entrance hall they heard Ingo's voice, disturbingly attractive, with a laugh in it. 'Where the devil is everyone? Genny? Trish? This is a lovely welcome, I must say!'

'We're in here!' said Genny, the only one who could possibly have found her voice. She could feel the thrill of emotion in the older woman, the strange remoteness leaving her finely boned face. She looked anguished, extremely vulnerable, so much so that Genny was seized with compassion. Trish was almost crouched at the other side of the room, as tormented in her fashion as was her mother. Genny's mind and heart leapt forward.

Ingo came in, so impossibly handsome, so vivid and authoritative that Genny could well understand his mother's spontaneous shrinking. He looked overwhelmingly sure of himself, perfectly made in his father's image except for his mother's eyes. Marianne's hands were clinging to her, seemingly trying to draw strength from Genny's young vitality. It seemed almost unforgivable that her dearest wish should not be fulfilled, infinitely pitiful that she should so expose herself to further pain.

Ingo had come to a halt in the arched doorway, as still as a statue, then he threw up his dark head exactly like a high-mettled thoroughbred, his eyes so brilliant, so furious that they could have slashed all of them to ribbons. A few feet away from him, her face paper-white, Trish rushed into speech:

'Please, Ingo, whatever you think, just be kind!'

He didn't even glance at her; kindness was not one of

his virtues at that time. His aura was remarkable, confusing them, his expression relentless, the mouth faintly contemptuous and proud as the devil. 'Genny!' he said, in a hard, impassive voice.

'I'm sorry. I'm sorry!' Trish began to cry, great tearing sobs she didn't bother to control.

The room was full of a bright hostility, a raw, aching sensitivity. Genny could feel her heart pounding. She could see no victory here for Marianne, who was extremely pale and staring with a peculiar fierce intensity at her only son. No one seemed to matter to her but Ingo, and he was burning with a bitter resentment. Genny had no real wish to, but she couldn't see what else she could do. She dropped Marianne's hand, patting it consolingly in the last second.

'I'm so sorry, Mrs Faulkner. Please believe me.'

Marianne didn't answer, her brilliant light eyes focused entirely on this forbidding near-stranger. It was costing her a considerable effort just to stand there unwaveringly, like a victim trying to face up to a firing squad. Ingo's stillness didn't deceive any of them. He was white under his tan, his eyes so glittery that they were as extravagantly beautiful as diamonds.

'I take it you're not coming, Trish!'

It wasn't a question but a statement and Trish realised what it meant well enough. 'But I wanted to. I *wanted* to!' she cried.

Her distress might have softened another man's heart, but her brother only turned his head and looked down at her crumpled in a chair. 'Why can't you leave well alone?'

'Please, Ingo, leave her!' Genny implored. 'I doubt if she knows.'

'Then I can't think why. I'm sorry to have to disappoint the children. It should have been an occasion. Perhaps another time.' He reached out his hand and locked his fingers about Genny's wrist, hurting her without knowing it, his body answering the icy outrage in his mind. Genny, looking up into his face, could see he was blind and deaf to any kind of entreaty; still she tried.

'Can't we take them? Can't we wait in the car? We've come all this way!'

'The blame is mine entirely!' Marianne Faulkner said, speaking for the first time to the son she had deserted. She sounded agonised, grief-stricken, all the ancient wrongs as fresh in both their minds as twenty years before. 'Ingo, can't you, *won't* you speak to me?'

'Forgive me, madam,' he said cuttingly, 'but I don't know you.'

'Why are you so heartless, Ingo?' his sister suddenly made a rush at him, pulling on his arm. 'You look like Father!'

'Get out of my way!'

The violence was in him and Genny started to tremble. It seemed to check him. He looked down at her, then put his sister's hand almost gently away from him. Trish's eyes had darkened to slate, her soft mouth working.

'Always Genny! Little Genny with the baby curls. I hated you, Genny, for years, but it was never your fault. You didn't ask for Ingo's cold heart, it was always yours —Mother and I are the beggars. You've marked us, you and Father, between you. What did you lose, really? You have Tandarro. Father cared for no one but you. I was nothing, a girl, expendable. Why don't you listen to the story of *my* life? Second best for everyone. Mother, Father, *you!* I was your sister, but it was Genny you always cared about. Where is she now? On Tandarro. It should have been my world, but *I'm* the refugee!' She suddenly rounded on Genny, driven by the demons of jealousy, only half exorcised. 'That's it,

Genny! Pansy eyes full of tears, pained little face, sexy as blazes. Compassionate little Genny and nobody's fool. He's in love with you, don't you know? No, don't stare at me. It's not ridiculous, I've known for years. That's history. Aren't you interested, or has he had you already?'

'Patricia!' The word whipped out in the most appalled protest.

Trish whirled around to her mother, blinking her eyes. 'Don't try and stop me now, Mamma. I've told you all about Genny. Forget the frills, the big eyes and the silver curls. I hate the sight of her. She's an opportunist, just like her mother.

Ingo's open-handed slap sent her reeling. She collapsed into a chair, sobbing bitterly, one cheek blazing hotly, the other tear-stained and deathly white. Genny gripped Ingo's hand, holding it tightly, afraid he might go even further. The flash in his eyes was startling.

'You shouldn't have done that!' she protested.

'She deserved it, the whimpering, whining little bitch. One should really convey one's congratulations to her mother. That's a splendid job of child-raising. A severe case of emotional instability!'

'Oh, please, Ingo!'

Marianne Faulkner went forward quietly, trying to comfort her daughter. 'She's only fighting for a little of what belongs to her.'

The furious passion was gone from Ingo's face. He was studying his mother and sister as though he had never seen them before in his entire life, and had no interest whatever in seeing them again. 'Really?' he said suavely. 'I thought you both received a more than generous settlement.'

'I'm talking about love!'

There was silence for a moment, then Ingo's contemptuous, humourless laugh. 'I'm sure your knowledge of the subject wouldn't amount to much!'

'We'll go, Mrs Faulkner,' Genny said wretchedly. 'Things can only get worse. I'm very sorry!'

'I just wanted to see my son!' Marianne Faulkner said in a heartbreaking voice, her back to them.

'So help me God, madam, you've seen him. Was it worth it?' Ingo demanded.

'*I* think so!'

'Come with me, Ingo. *Now!*' Genny whispered, not liking the infernally arrogant set of his head.

'Yes, go with her right into hell!' Trish burst out violently.

'It would be better than Paradise with anyone else!' Ingo said cruelly. 'I'll send you a postcard.'

It was like a nightmare and it had to come to an end. Genny lifted her head, listening. A door opened upstairs, then feet flew down the stairway, making quite a clatter. A moment later two excited young children appeared, a boy and a girl of seven and five, pausing in the doorway to catch their breath before they launched themselves at their uncle; their faces shining with pleasure, fair hair neatly brushed, hazel eyes reflecting their radiant happiness.

'Uncle Ingo!'

'Hi, kids!' Ingo said quietly, a hand on each shoulder.

Wrapped up in their own delight as they were, his subdued greeting wasn't quite the shock it might have been. 'Hello, Genny!' Both of them were dancing up and down in a near-frenzy of anticipation, Sarah, wondering why Uncle Ingo wasn't whirling her around as he usually did, Sean, the spokesman, telling them how great it was to see them.

'We're all ready!' he proclaimed happily. 'Mummy told us to wait upstairs for a while, but you were taking too long. What's in the box in the hallway?'

'The one you went mad about last time!' Genny smiled, trying to act naturally.

'Oh, boy!' both children said together, their sweet little faces regarding their uncle with love and pride. 'Aren't you going to get up, Mummy?' Sean asked.

'We're not going!' Trish said flatly in case her voice should break.

Sean looked round at her, his face charged with astonishment. 'You're kidding! We're all packed. I've done all my jobs and Sarah's drunk all her milk. We're longing and longing to go!'

'There's been a change in plan!' Trish answered abruptly.

'But we're *packed*!' Sean protested, not quite able to take the extraordinary news in.

Sarah's radiant little face suddenly crumpled and she broke into a wail that threatened to deafen them.

'You stop that!' her mother flared, feeling too weak to stand on her feet.

'Can't they come?' Genny rushed in on impulse. 'They're all ready. It seems so pathetic. I'll take very good care of them. Can't they come, Trish?'

Trish was stirred to maternal reconsiderations, her head bent, not looking at anyone. 'Sean can go!' she announced at last.

'Both or neither!' Genny said firmly, not having to bother about Sarah's reaction, for she had started up her distressing cry again.

'All right, take them!' Trish cried out emotionally. 'They don't want me either!'

'Show some good sense, dear!' Marianne Faulkner admonished her daughter quietly. 'The children have been so looking forward to this. They'll never forgive you.'

Trish laughed shortly, a queer little sound. 'I could never face *that*!' she said, her eyes bitter.

Ingo turned away from all of them, most definitely cutting the departures short. 'Show me your things, Sean. I'll put them in the car!'

'Yes, sir!' Sean raced ahead, pointing out two pieces of expensive luggage, one with a beautiful Victorian doll sitting on top, staring at them with her round brown eyes.

'Take the doll, son, Sarah better carry it!' Without a backward glance Ingo walked out to the car, hearing Genny's clear voice telling the children to 'Kiss Mummy and Nanna goodbye!' His mouth twisted with the irony of it. There was so much anger in his heart, yet Genny was incredibly tolerant, exquisitely compassionate for a girl who usually exulted in defying him. She could blaze and she could be so very, very tender. So many different things! He was disgusted with his sister. The urge to attack Genny on no provocation had proved irresistible: she really needed a psychiatrist. He had become very fond of the children, but if Genny wasn't out in a moment he wasn't going to wait.

She was there before he had even reached the car, Sean and Sarah clinging to either arm, Irene, the doll, not forgotten. 'Hop in, kids!' said Genny, opening the back door and seeing the children seated before she went to join Ingo, who was about to open the boot. He looked directly into her face, his silver eyes so keen that they seemed to be shooting rays of light through her.

'Damn it, she's hurt you, hasn't she?'

'Forget it!' she said wryly. 'Maybe she sees me like that.'

'And what is she, with all her petty little jealousies? I thought she'd stifled all that. Compared to you, she's led a charmed life!'

Genny touched her hand to her forehead. 'If anyone else makes a snide remark about my mother, I'll scream!'

'You can scream until you run out of breath, but it won't alter the truth. I could choke Flick for the dangers she's exposed you to.'

'What dangers?' she said, closing her mind on one or two unpleasant incidents.

'Don't give me that!' he said harshly, throwing the luggage into the boot. 'Take your hands away.'

'I can look after myself, Ingo!' she said, moving away.

'You don't know the first thing about yourself. Only poor old Hughie was a man of good sense and integrity —ah, forget it!' he bit out, his mouth hard. 'I've been worrying about you for years now.'

'I've come through all right, even if I've forgotten what it's like to have one joyous day. Besides, you always made your presence felt!'

'Someone had to!' he said bitterly.

'Please don't upset the children!'

'All three of you, you mean? Right!' he said, slamming the boot down. 'Let's get the hell out of here. It's wonderful to have such a delightful sister. My cup runneth over!'

'She can't help herself, Ingo. Go easy on her.'

'She's lucky I didn't murder her,' he retorted.

It wasn't until they were all seated in the car that Trish came to stand at the door, lifting her hand. The children responded, vaguely perplexed by the turn of events, but so alive and expectant that they unanimously rejected all adult complications. They were off on a lovely adventure, and Sarah was busy telling her doll all about it. Genny thought to raise her hand as well, but found she just couldn't. Her sense of charity had run out and she had only done it for the children anyway. Trish's accusations she didn't want to think about. Jealous frustration used any weapons. In some ways Trish was still, at twenty-eight, a maladjusted child. Genny stared before her, more hurt than she would ever admit. Ingo didn't even trouble to look towards his sister reversing the car with marvellous precision down the difficult sloping curve and out on to the road.

Marianne Faulkner had come to stand behind her daughter, trembling with misery but unable to forgo one last glimpse of her son. He was very like her husband and she saw it plainly, deeply disappointed in her daughter.

'That was unforgivable, Trish, the things you said. Were they really necessary?'

'God knows!' Trish said in a low, intense voice, humiliation flooding her. 'I wish I hadn't now. Did you see his face? He's very like Father and I make no apology for saying it. He'd throw us all to the lions for Genny. No man has ever looked at me like that or been ready to defend me in the same furious way!'

'My son is a man of strong passions,' Marianne said gently. 'I know now he will never forgive me. It couldn't be otherwise. I left him alone when he was only a boy. He'll never forgive me, no matter what Genny says.'

'And why should *she* plead your cause?' Trish demanded curtly.

'Because I can see right through to her soul. I had no idea she was so beautiful—I imagined her more like Felicity. Sweet, silly Flick, though I always liked her. Her daughter is a woman of a different calibre. It can't have been easy for her, not with those looks and Flick's way of life.'

'Oh yes, she's the flower child, all right. And so pure!'

'You should be grateful to her.'

'Never!' Trish maintained, pierced with hate. 'I don't know what Ian is going to say. He happily accep-

ted an invitation too, and his leave starts in tw[e]
None of them can see enough of Ingo!' Her th[
sharpened with misery. 'Including me!'.

'The pity of it all!' Marianne Faulkner turned
for the car had gone, and she stood in the hallw[
certain of where to go. 'We brought this all o[n
selves. Whatever was I doing here, Trish?'

The naked pain in her mother's face made Tris[
cover herself. She went tenderly to her, putting
arm about her mother's shoulders and leading
back into the living room. 'You said it yourself.
have a right to see your son.'

'No, Trish. No right. I gave that up years ago. N[
inevitably I have to bear the guilt and the pain.'

'Meanwhile Gen has Ingo, Tandarro, and [
children!' Trish said violently.

Her mother looked up, unwilling to add to h[
follies. 'Make an effort to help yourself, Trish. Y[
have no reason to speak this way about Genny. Wha[
ever you've told me at any time, I've always made u[
my own mind. Meeting Genny today has been som[e
thing of a revelation. She could be your friend. Do[
let your jealousy destroy everything that's good in y[
You have to save yourself. It could change your life.'[

'You don't understand, Mamma!' Trish said in s[
exasperation.

'Oh, but I do!' Her mother looked right through[
with her strange luminous eyes, so much like I[n
that Trish dropped into a chair, hiding her head. '[
been very good to us, despite everything.'

'Pride!' Trish maintained in a muffled voice.
Faulkner pride. Faulkner women good or bad do[
begging. He's been looking after Flick and Gen[
years. They're set to move in now.'

'Why did you let the children go?'

'I want them to know Tandarro.'

Marianne Faulkner closed her eyes in near-exhaustion. 'You want them to have Ingo's affection!'

'Genny can't have it all. There's a great yearning in me to be loved, Mamma. Ingo's always been a great part of my life. Even without him we've never been free of him or Father. It's a great sorrow we ever left our part of the world!'

'Well, my darling,' said Marianne Faulkner, her eyes swimming, 'we can't do anything about it now. Because of what I did, we all suffered. At the time it seemed all I *could* do. Marc had so little time to listen to my silly fears. His father never approved of me—Evelyn tried to be kind, but she was so under her father's influence. It was something that given maturity I would never do again, but I was never given a second chance. Marc loved me, but he was tired of what he thought of as my weakness. He never realised the extent of his father's antagonism. It was a sad story and you don't want to hear it again. Your father wasn't the hard and ruthless man you remember. He was a proud man and I hurt him badly. It seems extraordinary to me how I ever made such a terrible mistake. I should have stayed and triumphed and outwitted the old man. I should never have deprived Ingo of his mother, or you of your father and brother. Because of me—because of me . . .'

'Don't, Mamma, please. I feel nearly dazed with upset. The only good thing is Genny will look after the children!' And saying that, Trish suddenly broke into uncontrollable wild laughter, leaning forward in her chair with her arms tightly folded about her body. Happiness was a priceless gift. One should never dash it away with violent words.

CHAPTER SIX

IN the way of nightmares, the shock and distress of the incident in Adelaide didn't lessen and fall into unimportance with time. As the days slid by into weeks, Genny found herself becoming more and more affected by its memory. Trish had appointed herself some kind of executioner, killing all hopes of friendship between them. She flinched away from the cruel label so vehemently applied to herself and Flick, yet the word gave her pause. Ingo had been extremely generous to them both with his time and his money. He was, in fact, supporting them now. Did that automatically make them opportunists? Perhaps Marianne Faulkner thought the same thing as her daughter; Trish had obviously discussed them endlessly with her mother, Trish eaten up by jealous traumas, Marianne scarcely in the position to make a fair judgment, exiled as she was from Tandarro and all who came to be on it.

The whole incident had unwanted reverberations for Genny that she couldn't brush aside, coming between her and her appetite and her usual dreamless nights. She began to lose weight and laughed a lot less, a thousand doubts splintering round in her head. Of course she had given Flick and Aunt Evelyn a soft-pedal version of their visit and they had cast it aside, fairly used to Trish's uncomfortable little devils. The children were so engaging, their laughter so infectious that they were accepted at any price. Trish was often appallingly unreasonable, and no doubt she would write and apologise for her behaviour. No one wished to broach the subject of Marianne Faulkner. There was nothing anyone could do there. They had lived long enough with Ingo to realise that.

Trish did write her letter of apology, which Ingo read with irony and dumped in the waste-paper basket, obviously able to sublimate every last feeling, his dark face so aloof and solitary that Genny, who had been offered an apology as well, just turned away from him, her tender young heart bruised with the cruelty of it all. At such times she wondered if any woman could ever get close to Ingo again.

Despite the agonised tenor of Trish's letter, Genny was fairly certain that Trish would say the same things again, with probably a few more terrible comments. It didn't appear to bother Ingo, who had a fair sprinkling of saint and devil in him as well. He simply told Genny with a half-mocking smile that she could decide if and when Trish ever set foot on Tandarro again. Though the statement had been delivered with nonchalance, she realised he meant it. She realised too, and the knowledge came almost too late, that she would never escape him. Ingo *was* ruthless. Bitter, and disillusioned. She was also so much a part of him that the terrible meaning of it was love.

She was helpless now and she didn't really know what went on behind his handsome, sombre face. His hold on her was relentless, like a giant spider's web spun from childhood. She could no more prevent him from taking over her life than stop the sunrise. Both brilliant images were the everyday, ordinary things that she in her innocence had taken so much for granted. Ingo had a flair for directing lives. Hers he seemed to have engulfed completely, and it had been so easily achieved she had not been aware of it until now.

It was quite a relief to have Dave arrive, filling in her time. He was relishing his surroundings, very good with the children, expressing his pleasure so charmingly that Aunt Evelyn gave her unstinting approval: no small thing. Sally, who flew in a few days later, was not quite so popular with the household, which didn't really matter because she managed to keep herself very much by Ingo's side, riding out with him every day, beautifully turned out, even accompanying him on his weekly mercy visit to old Colonel Hastings' property, the Colonel having been a lifelong friend of Ingo's grandfather. Sally had settled in nicely, full of enthusiasm and ready peals of laughter, a complete contrast to Genny in every way, because Genny, to everyone's marked attention, had gone very quiet.

Dave, blissfully happy in her company again, found time to remark on it as they kept one eye on the children who were bathing in the crystal-clear shallow reaches of the Five-Mile lagoon. Every day they did something different, but the children always insisted on a swim first, not surprising in the dry heat. Genny was looking at the children too, laughing and splashing one another, as she used to do, her small face very much lost in thought and deeply introspective.

Dave caught her hand, grasping her fingers and nibbling on them. 'What are you thinking about, Gen?'

She turned to him apologetically, as though she realised now that the silence had gone on too long. 'I'm sorry. Had I gone off somewhere?'

'You know you had. The fact is, you've been very preoccupied since the day I arrived.'

'Oh, I'm sorry!' she said, touching his cheek briefly. 'I really want you to enjoy yourself.'

He looked at her, a very attractive young man who wanted to be with her exclusively. 'Sweetheart, don't think I'm complaining. I'm having the best time of my life. Close up to a great station I tell you it's terrific. People don't realise how different the life is. It's staggering, the size of the place, talking in thousands of square miles! Boy, that's awesome. It has to add some

141

extra dimension. Your cousin is no ordinary guy, that's for sure!'

'No, he isn't, now you mention it,' Genny said rather flatly.

'Very knowledgeable too about medical matters,' Dave added, genuinely admiring. 'Things must have been pretty grim before the RFDS. It's really something, isn't it?'

'Literally our lifeline. Most station people are very resourceful. They have to be, but we rely on our Flying Doctor. He makes all the difference between life and death, a friend and a link beyond price. One of Ingo's closest friends is Bob Melville, their top man, and he often drops in just to say hello. The Flying Sisters as well. People are very friendly in the Outback. There are so few of us, we cling together!'

'Yes, I suppose so. That's some medical kit you have.'

Genny nodded. 'We all have them. Each item is numbered. It makes it easy for the doctor. Some things can be treated at home—you've heard the mothers speaking to the doctor about their babies. That accident over at Lake Frome was a bad one, but even the most isolated station can contact a doctor within minutes, so you can imagine what it means to us. The women use the vast RFDS network for their galah sessions. It can be very comforting, their only link with the rest of the world. Can you imagine what it was like before that? The suffering and the needless tragedies? A small child dies very easily. Tandarro has a good few graves.'

'You're fortunate in your aircraft, though, aren't you? I mean, two private planes and a helicopter?'

'Ingo uses the Cessna and the helicopter for directing and supplying the mustering teams, inspecting the stock and the property, that kind of thing. You don't imagine he could ride over it, do you? We'd never see

142

him from one year to the next!'

'They must have cost a packet!' Dave persisted, fascinated by everything on the station.

Genny shrugged. 'They pay for it in performance. I think it costs the flying doctor planes in our sector alone about a thousand dollars a day, seven days a week, just to keep in the air. The Baron we use for city trips or functions on other properties, country race meetings, the occasional ball. We have functions here too as well. Isn't the ballroom terrific?'

'The whole place is unbelievable!' enthused Dave.

'There are other magnificent properties. This is the home of the cattle kings.'

'I have to hand it to them. That's just how they live!' Dave said enthusiastically, clearly unaware of the long hours, the hard work and the dangers involved. 'I guess your cousin would be a highly eligible bachelor?'

'He's that!' agreed Genny wryly.

'Not for long. Our Sally would like to put him in a cage.'

'How unimaginable!' Genny said, waving back the children. .

'It would be hard, I agree. Even a velvet one wouldn't hold him. He's kinda tough, isn't he? Super independent. The life style, I suppose—not very liberated towards women. You know, master of a great holding and the rest.'

'It isn't that. It's a man's world out here. It's our men who opened this country up. Their women made it habitable, fine brave women, but no woman has a man's strength and physical strength and endurance counts.' Genny smiled wanly. 'Besides, you know how men are. They find it easier to relate than women. Ingo grew up to a great heritage. He never knew anything else. He wouldn't even know how to be ordinary!'

'Wouldn't that make him kinda difficult to live with?'

'It makes him damned difficult to live without!'

'Well, Sally's a tryer. A little pushy but very slick and glamorous. I like her. Think she's got a chance?'

'Of what?' Genny asked, crushing a flower.

'Landing the million-dollar prize. Literally million-dollar, I imagine.'

'Sally's people are in a very big way!' Genny said, as though that answered something. 'Ingo wouldn't be a safe man to marry.'

'What is that supposed to mean?' Dave demanded, puzzled by the sombreness of her pure profile. 'I thought you two were very close. I know he adopts a very protective attitude towards you, maybe high-handed.'

'And that's why I'm saying it. Ingo is a very complex man. He's not like you, for example.'

'You could kiss me in grateful acknowledgment!' Dave suggested, not in the least playfully.

'The children may turn around,' she hedged.

'Oh well, later. Come to think of it I haven't kissed you properly once. In fact, I think you're taking very good care I don't. What's up, Gen? You know I love you. I want to marry you. It's my dream or my hang-up, I don't know which.'

'You know my views about marriage, Dave.'

'I've heard them. You're the original crazy mixed-up kid. Happiness isn't known to all that many, I agree, but quite a few prefer marriage to any other way.'

'I'm not scorning it, Dave. I'm just very wary.'

'Naturally!' said Dave, looking at her seriously.

'Don't say any more!' she pleaded.

'Sweetie, I wasn't going to. I'm greatly taken with your mother, as you know. I find it impossible to remember she's anyone's mother. In that outfit she had on this morning she looked Sally's age, maybe younger. She'll sure make her mark in Texas.'

'Why do you say that?' Genny demanded.

'Because it's true, little blossom. I've been here a week and I've had time to study Dan at close range. She's leading him around by the nose. Damned funny considering the size of him. Anyway, he's an improvement on Hughie.'

'You're not the first to say that,' observed Genny.

'I'll bet your cousin was the other. He's perfectly well aware of the set-up. Would anything escape those diamond eyes? God, aren't they lancing? The Chief has eyes like that, only they're blue. He doesn't like me much either.'

'Ingo does!'

'Yes!' Dave agreed in a very pleased voice. 'I had noticed his extreme hospitality, which doesn't mean to say he thinks I'm a suitable mate for you.'

She shifted uneasily. 'He hasn't said a word on the subject. Not that I see much of him.'

'He'll get around to it, never fear. I very much admire him, but I wouldn't like to cross him. I've noticed he's the kind of man that comes right out into the open. I think he might even chop me up into little pieces. I'd have a hard time getting his permission to carry you off, anyway.'

'I'm disappointed in you, Dave,' she said in a little jeering voice. 'I thought you'd just ignore Ingo!'

'Ignore him? You're kidding! That sort of man is impossible to ignore. Sneaking off wouldn't do any good either, he'd come right on after you. Don't misunderstand me, honey, I'm brave enough, but I'm not going to cross your cousin. Clearly he's more of a man than I am.'

Genny heard him with her heart twisting over. It was getting harder every day to keep up her own brave

145

front when she was feeling so vulnerable. It was true that she saw little of Ingo. She had deliberately been avoiding him anyway, unconsciously aided and abetted by Dave and the children, with whom she spent all of her time. Only at dinner did she see him for any length of time. He was gone early and he never came in for lunch, not even to please Sally. Genny's mouth twisted wryly. She had never been able to strike a balance with Ingo and these days he didn't seem to care. It was beautiful at the lagoon, a paradise with its perpetual sunlight, its native trees and the moon-shaped ring of clear, sparkling water, sloping from the shallows into very deep water. Like Dave, Genny had already been in for a swim and now the sunshine fell all over her, gilding her hair and her skin.

In her brief two-piece swimsuit, a stark black against her golden-tanned skin, she looked so unintentionally provocative, so delicately sensual, that Dave was beginning to feel the blood thundering in his head. Genny simply didn't know the pressures she put on a man. She was a highly intelligent girl, but she simply wasn't aware, nor made the slightest effort to promote her own highly inflammable female aura. She was, in fact, Dave considered, despite her luscious Italianate eyes and mouth, a very conservative girl, in no way as forward as any of the nurses he practically had to fight off, or so he thought to himself. There was plenty of communication at the hospital on a one-to-one ratio. In his experience Genny had never been known to make the first move, and in two years he had no more than kissed her deeply moulded mouth. All the same, it more than measured up to his other adventures, which naturally he didn't tell her about. They were not engaged or anything like that, not even a friendship ring, but Dave was unusually resolved to win a yes from her to his marriage proposal. A rising young doctor needed a wife. Maybe not quite so beautiful a wife; with such a face a few people might question her. As it turned out she was the most innocent girl he had ever known—unbelievable, he considered, with such a mother, who needed a man to love her like a swimmer needed air. It was a shame in a way Genny insisted on taking the children along on all their jaunts. Not that he didn't like Sean and Sarah, they were very entertaining and well behaved; it was simply that they never strayed off for even five minutes, and Dave was down to regarding five minutes as half a lifetime.

Something had happened to Genny. She was in some way changed, and so far he hadn't figured out what it was. She might almost have fallen violently in love, she was so lost in her own world, but it was fairly safe to assume that it wasn't that. There was only her cousin Ingo, who was a natural to arouse any red-blooded woman, but he was family. There was no mistaking his attitude towards Genny, and Dave had to respect it. Their relationship had gone right back to Genny's earliest childhood, so one could discount a cousin even if he did call the tune. Anyway, Sally was wild about him and ten times as experienced as Genny; delightful and enterprising, even if she didn't make the heart race like Genny, who was in the grip of some strong emotion he couldn't find out about.

She had worried for years about her mother, he thought. Perhaps it was that. She had had plenty of cause to worry too. Lovely dreamy Felicity was really a case, and a terrible judge of a man's character. At least the big American was a man one could like and admire. He was no fool either, even if he was acting like one at the moment. Once he put a ring on any woman's finger she would just have to behave.

Dave decided he would continue to prod. In another

ten minutes the children would come tearing up the sandy bank crying out for an apple or a cold drink or whatever. Everything and everyone on the station seemed to revolve around Faulkner, the centrifugal force. There was something significant in that. Dave knew there was a curious affinity between Genny and her cousin, something that seemed to imprison both of them, for he had seen them striking sparks off one another. Ingo Faulkner really posed an unfathomable question mark in Genny's young life. Dave felt immeasurably far from that kind of man, but not quite as effete as he imagined himself at the outset of this visit. He had acquired a very attractive tan, nowhere as deep as Faulkner's but attractive all the same. The nurses at the hospital would certainly comment on it to his advantage. He had even succeeded in getting one or two of them to fall in love with him. But they weren't Genny, that was the trouble.

'Please look at me, Gen!' he said softly, leaning over her and groaning aloud. 'You know, I'm barely able to keep my hands off you. You have the most beautiful skin—tactile. I feel kinda breathless.'

'I'd better put my jacket on,' she said prosaically.

'Don't. Anyway, it's see-through. What a miracle a woman's body is! Perfect. Perfectly formed for loving. But you don't, do you?' He tipped her dimpled chin to him and held it. 'You don't love me, do you, Gen?'

'What *is* love?' she asked, grave as a child, her dark eyes as deep as the far end of the lagoon.

'What I'm feeling right now!' Dave said in a husky voice.

'Couldn't that be physical infatuation?'

'Don't knock it, kid. It's rarer than you think.'

'Believe me, I'm not!' She shivered in the hot sun, still feeling the turbulence Ingo incited in her with just a glance.

148

'Don't you want to get married?' Dave asked, stroking her satiny shoulder.

'You're off your head!' she said, trying to smile.

'Damn it, sweetheart, that's no way to answer. Various young women of my acquaintance would be glad to be sitting right where you are now!'

'I'll bet. You have a way with the female person. Don't worry, I accept it. A good-looking young doctor —a big hospital—all those sex-starved nurses——'

'Believe me, it happens!' Dave said not unpleasurably.

'What are you trying to say—and leave your hand right where it is.'

'I want you to marry me!' he said in disgust. 'Dad is thinking of buying me into a private practice next year.'

'Why don't you join the Flying Doctor?'

'I'm not that brave. I like safe, city work. Except that it's so crazy I'd say you're in your cousin's clutches. Maybe you've even lost your head over him.'

'Ingo wouldn't stand for it!' Genny said, shaking her shining head.

'He's very important to you, though, isn't he?'

'Of course!' Genny said dryly. 'Have you ever seen anyone more splendid than Ingo?'

Dave shook his head. 'No, I haven't, and it disturbs me to admit it. I'm glad he doesn't work at the hospital. The nurses would ignore me. I know you share a special relationship with him, having known him all your life and being without a father or a brother. The pressures of your childhood, perhaps, a psychiatrist would say. Something has made you excessively wary of romanticising love and marriage, yet your cousin is altogether a very striking man. Deflationary for the rest of us. I mean he's extravagantly classy. Sally thinks so.'

Genny moved a little fretfully, pushing her fingers

149

through her drying curls. 'Let me nip all your terrible suspicions in the bud. Ingo and I aren't in the least bit romantic about one another.'

'Thank God for that!' Dave said piously, with very real feeling. 'I thought as much anyway. I mean, it's practically incestuous. Just thought I'd ask. It's really a very strange set-up altogether, his family I mean. His mother and sister living in Adelaide, his stepmother, the other one, what was her name? You did tell me.'

'Barbara. Uncle Marc married her on the violent rebound and ignored her from that day on. She was a very attractive woman but not very nice. As far as I can remember, she was all mushy about Ingo!'

'Great Scott!' Dave sat up straight, staring into Genny's face. 'You never told me that before.'

'You never asked. Ingo loathed her. In fact he tipped her out just as soon as he could. Ingo hasn't got much time for women.'

'Whatever it is that's bothering him, it's deadly with the ladies. I must try it some time.'

Genny smiled. 'You've had a very different life, Dave —peaceful, happy. Your mother and father adore you.'

'I know they think I'm more brilliant than I am.'

'Ingo was involved in endless running battles between his parents. Deep down he's as wary as I am. He'll be thirty-four next birthday and there's been a procession of Sallys. He's never married one of them.'

'Let's hope he does this time. I like her. She's great fun—a little too aggressive for my taste, but still fun. I suppose he wouldn't look sideways at a submissive little woman.'

'There aren't all that many of them around,' said Genny.

'No, I guess he'd go for sensuality and intelligence. Come to think of it, that's not Sally.'

'She knows exactly what she wants and how to get

ferocity. 'You've been looking like that
... art of two weeks.'
... ally?' she hurled at him at an equally low
... so urgent as when she was fighting him.
... easy, Giannina!' he warned her. 'It's been a
...'
... I thought you'd be enjoying yourself. Sally
... ttractive. Very obliging.'
... re thousands of women. I just don't want them
... the rounds with me. This used to be a fine, quiet
... Now for some reason I find it well-nigh impos-
... . I'm going over to Lake Frome to see how Jock is
... I'm leaving almost immediately. Want to come?'
... Why would you want me?' she asked.
'As a matter of fact I want to talk to you. It seems as
... we haven't talked in years.'
'Sally will be pretty much put out!' she said un-
certainly.
... Well, that's not going to change my mind.'
'What about Dave?'
'He can just hang in there with Sally, though it's a
pity to separate you. Let her supervise the kids for an
hour or two. It will make a nice change.'
'I promised them I'd take them to the caves.'
'Sally knows the way,' returned Ingo uncompromis-
ingly.
'I don't think she'll want to.'
'I guess you haven't heard,' he said curtly, his face
and his lean body oddly taut. 'I'm used to getting my
own way.'
'I know you act in a certain manner,' she retorted.
'Coming?' he asked, his brilliant eyes resting on her
face.
'Yes.'
'Why whisper it?'
'That's how I feel.'

it,' she rejoined. 'Unlike most men Ingo doesn't respond to the usual tactics. I've said all along she should
give him a bit of his own medicine. This has been
going on for years. Sally's Trish's age. She's more determined than most.'
'Think how deliciously exciting it would be to be
married, Gen!' he said, appraising her in a slightly
dangerous fashion.
'Plenty of people wish they'd never got married.'
'Your mother does it all the time. Whoops!' he hit
a hand to his forehead. 'I'm sorry I said that.'
'In a way, I don't blame you. Flick is different. She
can make easy undemanding relationships. Even when
she marries them she doesn't get very deeply involved. I
wish she'd been different, but I love her all the same. If
she does decide in favour of Dan I think my heart
would break.'
'Why, for God's sake?' Dave asked, grabbing her
hand.
She shook her head, not even able to answer him.
Overcome with tenderness at that point, he kissed her
cheek. 'Umm!' He moved his mouth from her cheek to
her chin and back again, aware of what was going to
happen in a few moments. Genny was the most exciting
girl in the world for him. Even kissing her cheek seemed
to melt him.
'Dreadfully sorry to interrupt!'
The gay ringing voice came from further up the
bank. They both looked at one another, then turned
their heads, Dave with barely disguised frustration,
Genny just as empty as she could have been. Sally was
making her way down to them, slithering a little on the
loose pebbles, Ingo a few feet behind her with absolutely no expression on his face.
'Sorry, kids!' Sally said, joining them. 'We were
riding this way, so we thought we'd look in. What a

beautiful spot! Makes me sorry I haven't got my bikini.'

'Me too!' said Dave, determined to be friendly.

Ingo didn't say anything for a minute, and instinctively Genny reached for her jacket and elbowed into it. It wasn't really practical even if it was very chic, for it was made of multi-coloured georgette.

'Hi!' Dave said, looking back to him with not the slightest idea of what he was going to say next. Really, did kissing Genny make all that much difference?

'You'd better get the kids out of the water, Genny,' Ingo said crisply. 'I think they've had enough sun for today.'

Genny stood up and looked at him, then moved down to the water's edge calling to the children. They waved and splashed the water at her, but they didn't make a move to come out. She hesitated only a moment, then plunged in after them, grabbing each by the hand and towing them to the bank. 'Uncle Ingo thinks you've had enough sun. We'll dry off and go home for lunch. After Sarah has a little nap we'll go and look at the caves.'

'Oh, beaut!' Sean exclaimed, crying out his heart with the expression, then he whooped like an Indian and ran on up to his uncle, pouring out the events of the morning, and all the pretty coloured stones they had found.

Sally made no pretence of listening indulgently to a child's excited rambling, starting up a conversation of her own with Dave, leading him down the stream to where the beautiful highly perfumed lilies swayed gently in the breeze. She plucked one and held it up to him while he showed a becoming interest. Genny, meanwhile, picked up a towel to dry Sarah off before pulling on her smock, Sarah all the while making big hazel eyes at her uncle, who was something of a fantasy figure to her.

'There you are, darling!' Genny said affectionately.

'Better put your hat on no[...] if you freckle that prett[...]

'I don't care!' Sa[...] Genny's nose. 'I think [...] Melissa has so many fre[...] really skin!'

'Melissa is a redhead, isn't [...]

'Yes.'

'Well, it's important for redhe[...] hot sun. Sean?' she turned her hea[...] Ingo.

Sean came obediently trotting down [...] picked up his tee-shirt, pulling it over his [...] ing back his hair that was curling in damp [...] your cap on like a good boy. Now the two o[...] up your things. You can use my straw hat to [...] your stones if you like.'

'Thanks, Genny.'

'You're not staying,' Ingo said in a voice that made her frown, as he came to join her.

'Is that a question or an order?' she flared abruptly.

'Why do you always exaggerate?'

'I know you, Ingo!' she said darkly. 'You'll frighten poor old Dave away'

'Sally can take care of him for a moment,' he said.

'Your loss?' she asked sarcastically.

'My gain!' he said with mocking contempt.

'Gosh, what a callous man you are!'

'Certainly. Did I ask Sally to come here? Answer quickly.'

'I'll have to. They'll come back at any minute.'

He was standing in her way and she had to look up at him, moving inexorably a little nearer him instead of away. His eyes seemed to be blazing in his darkly tanned face, coldly accusing her of something. 'You look as if you're about to burst into tears!' he said with

'You're pretty overwrought these days. I don't know whether to beat you or make violent love to you!'

Inexplicably the tension seemed to have died away in him. His hand dropped to her shoulder, unconsciously caressing the side of her neck with the tips of his fingers. 'You know, I envy your friend in a way.'

'He's been busy envying you!' she said wryly.

'No one would want my job. It's a twenty-four-hour day, plenty of grinding decisions. I feel jaded, sick to death of it all. I just want to check Jock, then that's about it. It was a near thing. Young Chris will be in hospital for weeks.'

'Shall you tell them where we're going?'

'Why not? I guess I'm entitled to your company once in a while.'

'I didn't know you wanted it lately.'

'I want it. I just don't advertise like your friend.'

'Well, I'm fairly important to him,' she pointed out. 'He wants to marry me.'

'That's damned nice of him!' His hand slipped to her nape, turning her head. 'A pity a *no* is inevitable!'

'Are you sure?'

'You'd better be!'

'You're hurting me,' she complained.

'Not nearly enough. I'd like to make you cry out!'

She swayed a little under his hand, shivering slightly like the leaves of the trees. She was stirred and excited and he knew it, deliberately tantalising her. 'What, no protest?' his voice mocked her. 'I could mean almost anything!'

'Well, I know you're capable of a little primitive action.'

'And you'll do *just* as I say.'

She gave a sad little laugh, blinking her thick lashes rapidly. 'Don't I know it!'

'Genny?' he asked abruptly, not surprised to see the

tears standing in her eyes. '*Genny*.' His voice fell to a level that made her avert her head quickly. There was a charged little silence and his hard cool fingers closed about her wrist. 'The times you pick! They're coming back, so act the little heroine. You can cry all over me later.'

Genny lifted her head to see Sally and Dave strolling back towards them, Sally with the lily in tow, obviously kidding Dave about something because he was laughing, a nice friendly laugh, unfeigned and spontaneous. Sally looked towards them and blew a kiss.

'I like your guy, Genny! When will congratulations be in order?'

'As it turns out, Sally, they're just good friends!' Ingo said lightly.

'So *you* say!' Sally chided him playfully, a small mocking reprimand on her face. 'I don't know how Genny tolerates you for a bodyguard.'

'She hasn't got much choice.'

'I'm beginning to believe that!' Sally answered seriously. 'You know, you're nearly a tyrant with the kid. What did you used to call him, Gen?'

'Black Ingo. I still do.'

'With some motivation. You two are unnecessarily complicated cousins.'

'Still, we're very fond of each other!' Ingo said suavely. 'I'm taking Genny over to Lake Frome this afternoon. Think you two could stand in as foster-parents for an hour or two?'

'Why, sure!' Dave said quickly, only too anxious to please.

'You could come, Dave,' Ingo said smoothly, 'only I won't be staying long and it's not really the time to take you visiting. They're all pretty much upset. Genny said you were going to show the children the caves. Sally knows the way!'

'Sally here is not too happy about it!' Sally announced. 'No offence, Dave boy!'

'Come right out with it!' he invited, smiling, enjoying her slight embarrassment.

'No, really!' she smiled back at him, liking the way his eyes crinkled. 'All right, Ingo Faulkner, since you always get your own way, Dave and I will play it smart and do what we're told.'

'You might even enjoy it,' he remarked.

'Actually I'm very interested!' Dave said, beginning to resign himself to the idea. Sally dressed in her prettiest gear wouldn't be a patch on Genny, but he liked her long sable-coloured hair and her thick creamy skin. He wouldn't be lonely at any rate. He was more in love with Genny now that she had been away from him than ever before.

The children came back and accepted the change in plans without question, whirling about like dervishes when Ingo said they could come back on the horses, Sarah with him, and Sean up in front of Sally, who was an expert horsewoman. Genny and Dave followed in silence; Dave determined not to brood, Genny with her feet flying so that she arrived back at the jeep breathless. Every minute alone with Ingo invited complications, but a subtle excitement was taking possession of her. It would be good to share the few promised hours with him, *so* good, Dave was left reflecting on the sudden blaze of light that had entered her face, taking the place of her former faint melancholy. She was beautifully animated now and he desperately wanted to take her in his arms, but he wasn't so blind that he couldn't see he wasn't the cause of it. Perhaps he had misread the whole situation.

When they met again for dinner it was quite an occasion, on two counts. First, Genny seemed miraculously restored to her usual good spirits, and Sally, who was an accomplished and adventurous cook, insisted on preparing the dinner, considerably ruffling Maggie's feathers in the process but charmingly uncaring. For a very glamorous and much travelled young woman, Sally was secretly burning for domesticity and was perfectly well able to run the domestic affairs of a great station.

One delicious course succeeded another, each suitably applauded, with Sally showing a characteristic lack of modesty regarding her own skills. Conversation never flagged for a minute, an unthinking compliment to such a beautifully prepared and presented meal and remarkably good wines, red and white. Dave was convinced he was dealing with a family who didn't live like ordinary mortals, and right at that moment the life seemed eminently desirable.

He had been staring at Genny with unconcealed lavish admiration, as Ingo later put it, 'devouringly'. Tonight she was wearing a dress the colour of his mother's prize hydrangeas, the most beautiful, lambent blue into violet, a smoky, flyaway sort of dress that left her arms and shoulders bare and revealed tantalising little glimpses of the shadowed cleft of her breast. Her huge dark eyes were faintly touched by the same blue above the thick mesh of her lashes and her silky curls formed a brilliant aureole around her warmly tinted face. Dave found himself having a hard time controlling his rapt feelings, not realising how much they were showing. Genny had such a living, breathing beauty, he would have been stone if he couldn't appreciate her.

Exquisite and disciplined as her mother undoubtedly was—Sally too, glowing with health, her tall svelte figure shown to great advantage in a seamless jersey—Genny easily outclassed both of them. Dave wished himself away from the scene and alone with her, preferably in some oasis in the desert, though he was enjoying himself and contributing in no small way to the conversation.

Faulkner, too, seemed to have undergone some subtle change. He was seated at the head of the table, immensely vital, graceful as a big cat and just as dangerous so far as Dave was concerned. There was an arrogant sureness about the man that Dave would dearly have liked to borrow. He was smiling now with lazy appreciation at something Sally had just said, his light eyes quite startling in so dark a face, fairly blazing, really, his crisp, thickly waving hair a true black. He looked, Dave considered, exactly how he should look against such a background, and was struck anew by the dynamic energy that radiated from him like an aura. It didn't make Dave all that comfortable, but he knew he would just have to suffer it, glad that he was in no kind of competition with Faulkner for Genny's fair hand. That would be like pushing a miracle.

No one seemed able to drag themselves away from the table, and discussed various subjects, serious and frivolous; even Aunt Evelyn was seen to smile frequently, to Dave's astonishment. He had come to the conclusion that she was a very formidable lady, almost unapproachable, like a Russian grand duchess, with a very cultivated voice that made Dave frequently want to check his accent. Tonight she didn't seem too bad at all, a handsome woman really, even witty in an archaic kind of way. Genny was obviously fond of her, so he would have to watch his step there. There was so much to learn that he was beginning to lose his confidence like a new ambassador at court, uncertain whether he would be accepted or fired out of the window.

Dan, who actually shared Dave's opinion of Miss Faulkner, was nevertheless attempting to explain

American politics to her, agreeing with her that the world owed an enormous debt to Britain for just about everything. Aunt Evelyn represented in herself the sheer eccentricity and the strength and the reliability that the British were famous for, and Dan just gave up, recognising that the competition was too strong. He looked towards Felicity as though they had some given signal arranged between them. Felicity smiled at him, then made a delicate little movement of her hand indicating that she wanted silence and cutting short Aunt Evelyn's examples of British heroism and other much admired sterling qualities, her delicately chiselled face as flushed as a rose.

'Dan and I have something important to tell you!' she said in her soft delightful voice, looking about the table. 'We've decided to get married!'

Dave reacted diplomatically, moved to mumble something vaguely congratulatory at the precise moment that Genny, exquisitely careful of every last Faulkner possession, knocked over her beautiful wineglass with its long fragile stem. It fell and splintered against the heavy silver centrepiece, bringing Faulkner to his feet.

'Leave it, Genny!'

She didn't seem to hear him, automatically attempting to gather up the pieces. Blood spurted from a finger and she pulled up her trembling hand, nursing it like an injured bird.

'I told you to leave it!' Ingo moved around to her. 'Melly will clean it up. Ring that bell for me, Sally. It connects with the kitchen. That didn't work out wonderfully well, did it, Flick? Couldn't you have waited until lights out?' While he was speaking he had bound a handkerchief around Genny's hand, drawing her unresistant out of her chair. 'Excuse us for a moment. We won't be long, then you can pick up where you left off,

160

Flick. Genny seems to have sustained some slight injury.'

'Who's the doctor in the house anyway?' Sally suddenly demanded, swinging about from ringing the bell.

'Anyone can cope with a Band-aid!' Ingo said blandly, as though she didn't really deserve an answer. 'I can't think why you didn't give us a warning, Flick.'

'I wanted to surprise you!' said Flick, her blue eyes concerned and infinitely bewildered.

'I sure hope you're pleased about it and all,' Dan said, like a child not wanting to have his pleasure spoiled.

'Of *course* we're pleased!' Ingo informed him. 'We're on your side, Dan. You may be able to do a great deal of good with her. Flick's a big girl now. My sincerest congratulations to you both, and my best wishes right from the jump. Ev, what about ordering up a bottle of champagne? Make it two if you like. The very best!'

'Well, I won't say no to it!' Sally announced gaily, not giving a damn if Felicity got married again or not. 'Can I get it, Ingo? I know my way around the murky depths of the cellar. Dave, you can come too, in case there's a spider or two. You haven't seen the cellar, have you?'

'Not so far!' Dave murmured, still unhappy about Genny, but lacking the brute strength to separate her from her cousin.

'Then you're in for a treat!' Sally said, taking him by the hand. 'It's better stocked than a lot of our best pubs.'

'What did she say?' Aunt Evelyn asked icily.

Nobody answered her, Ingo moving with Genny towards the door. 'Keep up the conversation, Ev, like a good girl. What about starting off with the Roman invasion and working through to 1066? We'll be back in a moment!' Out in the entrance hall he spoke to

161

Genny sharply. 'Don't you faint on me!'

'I'm not going to!' she said in a fierce little whisper.

'I hope not. That's only a very little cut!'

'Am I moaning?' she inquired.

'No, you've just gone as white as a sheet.'

'Shocks can be unpleasant.'

'Certainly, but that was no shock. Only the timing. Flick's an ass, she always has been.'

'I can't even talk about it.'

'That's obvious!' Ingo paused at the door of the first aid room, flicking on the light.

'Well, of course you don't give a damn!' Genny said, walking in and leaning back against the table.

'You're right about that! For myself I'd shoot Flick off on a one-way rocket to Mars.'

'Doubtless she's worn you down too,' she returned. 'You'll just have to forgive me if I feel a little sick. I love my mother—she's the only mother I've got. I don't want her to fly off to the other side of the world, let alone Mars!'

'Come over here to the basin!' he said, ignoring her tragic face. 'Cheer up, baby, I just might permit you to visit her for the occasional holiday.'

She held out her hand to him, shuddering. 'Nothing is ever going to be the same again.'

'I sincerely hope not! The past hasn't exactly been a ball game. That's it—hold your hand away from your dress. I wouldn't like to see it spoiled, neither would Dave. He's been devouring you for the past hour. It's quite put my teeth on edge. I'm even considering establishing my true position beyond doubt!'

'And what's that?' she asked, grimacing as he wound a Band-aid around her finger.

'Oh, that I'm your dreadful barbaric cousin and I won't even let you talk to another man.'

'I'm only sorry he's not bigger than you,' she said.

'Oh? Would you like to see me get a punch in the nose? It won't happen.'

'I know,' agreed Genny, 'Dave's unlikely to attack you anyway. I wouldn't know about Sally. Oh, what am I going to do? I don't think I can go back to the dinner table.'

'Yes, you can!' he said, giving her a challenging look. 'You may feel a little sick as you say, but you can take it on the chin quite as well as I can. Can't you, Giannina?' He turned her face up to him, looking down at her.

Her lids fell. 'No, I can't!' she said distractedly. 'I want to cry my eyes out, all huddled in a ball.'

'I'll join you.'

'That's good to know.' She fell forward, resting her head against him, feeling his arms link about her waist. 'I can't take it. *I can't!*'

'Then go with her.'

'I'm tired of living with my mother's husbands!' she groaned.

'Maybe you'd sleep better with one of your own.'

'Not for years yet!'

'Want to bet?'

She took no account of his mocking words, turning her head along his chest. 'Just keep holding me. Sometimes you frighten me so much it's pitiful, and other times I feel there's no safer place in this world than right here in your arms.'

'*Well!*' he jeered softly, his laughing breath stirring the tips of her curls, his arms closed about her lean and strong. 'That couldn't have been easy for you to admit!'

She nodded. 'Shocks can be disarming.'

'Can't they! Especially for girls like you. We can't stay here, Giannina. Flick's longing to fill us in with the rest of her plans. No doubt a civil ceremony in the garden at sunset. What could be more romantic than that?'

'Oh, shut up!'

'Turn your face up. I want to see if you've got your colour back.'

She lifted her head, feeling as fragile as an invalid. 'It's going to be an ordeal. Dear God, let her be doing the right thing!'

Ingo grunted. 'If we've got to speak of ordeals, it's been very trying watching Dave fighting to keep his hands off you. I'd have expected a doctor to have more control.'

'Has he really?' She looked up at him in a mystified way because he had spoken a little shortly.

'Didn't I warn you about my jealous streak?'

'I can't accept you'd apply it to me.'

He gave a savage little growl, akin to resignation. 'For a clever girl you're not exactly blessed with the good old-fashioned womanly perceptions. In fact I'm certain you don't know what being a woman is all about. All your gifts are natural, a handout from the Good Fairy. Unworked on. You're as unconscious of yourself as when you were ten years old. You don't even recognise flirtation. Sarah is more of a vamp than you are!'

'Why should that incite you to rage?' she asked.

'Who's raging? You'll know about it when I do. We'll both go up in a blue flame. Oh, come quickly!' he groaned. 'I wonder why I start these conversations!'

Genny did her best, but the rest of the night seemed frightful, the champagne not helping, not that she was over-fond of it anyway. It seemed incredible to her that yet another man had captured Flick's heart; worse still to realise that Flick was fully prepared to leave her. In fact she felt just like a parent whose favourite daughter just announced she had every intention of settling down in Africa. Though he had not been prepared in advance, Ingo's imaginative suggestion for a civil ceremony in the garden coincided with Felicity's dearest wish, and not at some future date but as soon as possible; Dan had assured her that she didn't have to bother her pretty little head about anything from that day forward. The house, the furniture, her now no-account clothes, could go up in flames.

Felicity, it now seemed, couldn't wait to rearrange her life with the Rio Grande somewhere in sight. It was not the first time Genny had felt desperately hurt by her mother, but she accepted that her mother was quite free to lead her own life. Suddenly she could stand no more of it, and got up from the table without an 'excuse me' feeling stupidly and unnecessarily sentimental in the light of Felicity's shining new happiness. Inside her room she locked her door carefully, but no one came near her, leaving her alone with her hurt. By the morning she would be over the worst of it until the actual day of the wedding.

Even as she thought about it her eyes filled with tears and she flung herself down on the bed, telling herself that mothers and daughters separated every day. Probably in six months' time Flick wouldn't even remember her.

CHAPTER SEVEN

GENNY didn't know what time it was, she only knew her head was pounding. Exhausted by a storm of feelings, she had somehow fallen off to sleep. Inertly she lay there for a moment staring up at the floral print of the bed canopy, then she slipped off the bed, padded to the dressing table and looked for her watch. There was a very old English grandfather clock right outside her door and two nineteenth-century wall clocks in her room, but none of them were concerned with accuracy as they gracefully ticked away at their own rate, dreaming of distant times and places.

It was well after midnight. Genny could scarcely believe it. She put her watch down with a gentle thump, her hand moving to the curve of her shoulder, rubbing it where the thin strap of her dress had cut into the soft skin. She really should have taken her dress off, but she hadn't expected sleep to rise up and engulf her. Night after night for the past weeks her mind had been a mad spinning top, throwing off all the events of the day and things from the past best not remembered or brooded over.

At least she hadn't left the chandelier blazing, only the winged companion bronze figures, male and female, that each held a bright electric flame aloft. She rarely suffered from headaches, but she had a bad one now. She caught sight of herself in the mirror and held her own gaze rebelliously. Obviously she had failed to take it on the chin in true Faulkner tradition. Now she had plunged them all into differing degrees of embarrassment. All except Ingo, who was impervious to the ordinary prevailing emotions. He would only be irritated. It was Dan she had really deprived of the pleasure of his big moment, probably tarnishing his memory of it for ever. Poor Dan! If he was to be believed, and instinctively Genny did believe him, this was his first love. It hadn't really been fair to race away from the table like that, yet she doubted even now if she could have stayed there. If only Flick had told her when they were alone! She would have been glad of that—glad of a few moments to collect herself in private, unexposed to everyone's eyes. Flick, smiling, showing her shining little teeth, delicate high cheekbones flushed. Flick, her mother!

Genny stared sightlessly into the fireplace, filled in the summer time with a magnificent brass jardinière containing various beautiful indoor plants. This week it was the gorgeous hippeastrum lilies, all their spectacular large flowers open. She would have to get something for her headache. She didn't think she could suffer it unaided. Comforting sleep would be impossible from now on. She felt wide awake and back to her profound depression. One never felt closer to a loved one than when they were going away. Flick could do just as she liked, and Genny wished her nothing but a lifetime of happiness; still the pain wouldn't go away.

Wall brackets lent the long gallery a dim glow. Faulkner men and women stared down from their gilded frames. The lights were always left on when there were guests in the house who were unfamiliar with switches and the size of the place. Genny made her way along it very stealthily though her stockinged feet made no sound at all, not even a whisper. She couldn't have borne to see anyone. She almost ran down the stairs, hugging the wall, then paused uncertainly just outside the library. Someone was moving about. Her heart gave a dismal lunge and she moved back under the staircase and into the shadows. She didn't want to see anyone. *Anyone!* She put her hands over her face and when she raised it again, an arm had closed about her.

'I suppose you know I thought you were a ghost?' Ingo swore so softly it was almost inaudible.

'Did I frighten you?'

'No. It's unforgivable, I know, but I'm not frightened of ghosts either. Just a momentary freezing shock. Come on out of there, you ridiculous child. It's well after midnight and you're still in your dress. What's the problem?'

'I have the most appalling headache,' she confessed.

'I'm not surprised. Apart from our news flash, you drank far more than you're used to. Don't let's wake the rest of the household, for God's sake. I couldn't stand it. Go into the study. I'll bring you a couple of tablets.'

'God bless you!' she said wryly, walking towards the glimmering light.

The study door was open, the tall standard lamp illuminating the leather jackets of the books in the ceiling-high wooden shelves. It was a very inviting sort of a room. She had always liked it, its proportions reduced by its masculine colour scheme and its deep comfortable furnishings. She wandered across to the sofa upholstered in a dark plaid and sank down on to it, leaning her head back and closing her eyes. If Ingo didn't mind, she just might sleep there, and as she thought that, she arranged two plump cushions under her elbow. With a little help from the tablets, she could get a few more hours' sleep and be ready to apologise in the morning for her mysterious behaviour. Her mother would accept it, her face full of genuine loving concern. It was truly strange, the different levels of loving, the deeps and the shallows.

Ingo, coming back into the room, looked down at her small, still face. It had on it an expression of faint mystic revelation that made him smile when he didn't feel in the least like smiling. 'Here, take these, Genny!' he said, bending over her.

Her eyes flew open and she took the tablets from him, letting him hold the glass. 'You said I could take it on the chin.'

'I was wrong,' he admitted.

'There's no need to rub it in. Where have you been? You've changed your clothes.'

'My dear child,' he said rather wearily, 'while you've been crying your heart out and sleeping like an exhausted child, I've been putting a fire out.'

'*Where?*' she said urgently.

'One of the saddle sheds. Someone was careless, but they'll hear about that in the morning.'

'But I never heard a thing!' she said disbelievingly. 'Not a sound. I'm sorry!'

'Why? What would you have done? Fight right along with me?'

'Did it do any damage?'

'It could have done. A good thing Spook is always roaming around.'

'Doesn't he ever sleep?' she queried.

'I understand he doesn't need it. But he does do a good day's work, that's all that matters. Remind me to get him some of that special pipe tobacco. Swallow those, will you, instead of looking at me big-eyed!'

Genny accepted the glass of water humbly, washing the rather large tablets down, her face relaxing after she had done so as though relief was guaranteed. 'I'm going to spend the night here. All right with you?'

'I wonder,' he murmured.

'I suppose Dan was upset?' she pursued.

'Yes, he was. For a man in middle life, Dan is as excited as a boy. It's touching, really.'

'And Flick?'

'Flick thinks you're entitled to a few tears. You know, routine!'

'You're a sarcastic devil! Remember when she told us she was going to marry Hughie?'

'I recall your pushing a chair over then, too!'

'So I'm making a fuss about nothing?'

'I suppose that's what it is, considering. You've had plenty of experience,' he pointed out.

'And just as Evvy was going on about sterling qualities. I feel I've let the team down.'

His brilliant eyes were moving over her face, and her slight graceful body. 'Evvy, my lamb, is on your side. She always has been. Besides, she's not in the least romantic!'

'How do *you* know?'

'I'd offend you if I told you.'

'She has a jumble of letters in a lacquer box in her room. Could they be love letters? You don't know everything.'

'Actually they're the daily dictates Grandfather sent her on his trips home to England.'

'Oh no!'

'Oh yes.'

'Poor Evvy. Aren't we all dominated?' she asked cheerlessly. 'Look up there at Uncle Marc!' Her glance darted towards the big portrait of Ingo's father.

Ingo didn't turn his head. 'What are you trying to say, little captive?'

'Something foolish, probably. You're very much like him—relentless, I guess it is. One-track!'

'And you want to change me?'

'At least about one thing. Now you're angry!'

'How do you know?'

'I can tell by your eyes. They shoot little sparks. Tell me, how did you all part tonight?'

'Properly!' he said, looking down his straight nose at her. 'About half-past ten. Naturally Dave was upset to lose your company, but then it wasn't offered. Such a pity he can't stay for the wedding. Flick asked him, but hospital rules, you know. He has to get back.'

'I don't want to talk about it.' Genny snatched up another cushion and hid her head in it, curling her legs under her and drawing right back to one corner of the sofa.

'Then it's going to be quite a struggle. Evv won't talk about it either, and I'm damned if I'm going to take time off to arrange any ceremony.'

'I said *stop*!'

'Who are you giving orders to?' He dropped down to the sofa beside her, his touch far from gentle.

She shook her head helplessly, a little unnerved.

'How's the headache?' he asked abruptly.

'It's a little better—and you don't have to speak so sharply.'

'Oh, but I do! So don't go trying to pick a quarrel.'

'It's too late for that,' she said, turning her head around, her glinting curls ruffled.

'So it is. Come here to me, Genny.'

'So you can tell me what to do?' Resignation edged her soft wail. 'Don't worry, I'll arrange it. You're paying, of course. Really, you know, Trish had a point.'

'Come here!' he said forcibly and lifted her with almost casual strength right into his arms. 'It looks as if I'm running out of patience.'

'What's it feel like?'

'Violent,' he snapped.

She lifted her hand and touched Ingo's face, her fingertips tracing the curve of his mouth, her feelings now so intense, so naked that they must have been shining out of her eyes. 'Life would be impossible without you, violent or not.'

'And intolerable *with* me? That's my impression.'

'You're a very hard man!'

'Sure.' His beautiful mouth twisted. 'I can dispense with everyone. Except you.'

'Why, why am I so important?' She spoke softly but intensely, her dark eyes searching his face.

'You've got a tenacious hold on me, Genny. Infiltration from your earliest days. You shouldn't really have come down, you know. The rest of the world seems far removed from me right this minute.'

His low voice, dark and faintly mocking, filled her with flame. 'What do you want from me?'

'So help me, more than you seem able to give. Where's

171

the fright in your eyes? I don't see it.'

'It's not there,' she said softly.

'It should be.'

Her head was tilted back over his arm, her shoulder curving to the palm of his hand. 'Love me, please, Ingo. *Love* me.'

She could feel the tautness in him, his brilliant eyes sweeping her face. 'I don't think you know how deep my feelings go. I can't love you as I want to without taking you completely!'

She looked back at him a little breathless. 'I didn't know you felt like that.'

'Don't be such a little fool. You said yourself I'm capable of anything.'

'But I *want* you to!' she cried, with the shocking realisation that it was true. 'I don't care!'

'But I do. *I* care.'

'Oh, Ingo, let me stay here!' She drew down his head inexorably, her mouth lifting to meet his, parted, her dark eyes so ardent and so eager that an escape route was closed and he lowered his head, his mouth closing over hers with such hunger that it fully aroused her to her own desperate desires. She couldn't have been nearer to him as surrender swept over her in a blinding, drowning rush, driving her past all thought of discretion or danger, the age-old primitive longings powerfully asserting themselves, satiated only in true culmination. All these deep-running yearnings were only to give her whole person to this one man she loved. She couldn't even attempt to deny him.

Lights seemed to be sparkling inside her head, brilliant lights, a myriad sensations that fused the two of them together. It might have been a fantastic dream, only these insistent demands were very real. Now when Ingo's hand touched her burning skin, closing over the tilted curve of her breast, resistance was beyond her, unreachable, unthinkable when this convulsive ecstasy was leaving her strangely urging him to take her. All her life, it seemed to her, this was what she had been searching for. All she had ever been or would ever be was Ingo's.

The rather high-pitched little moan was her own, and her heart beat with a wild abandon. She didn't want him to stop even when she felt she could bear it no longer. All a young girl's secret dreads were lost in desire, pleasure so piercing it mounted to torment. It was intolerable to go this far and not be engulfed—she wanted to find him, find him in the place where he lived all alone. She loved him and denied him any solitary corner of his soul.

Words seemed to jangle in Genny's head. A voice . . .

From delirium she was brought back to a confusing, swirling present. Ingo still held her, one hand shaping the back of her head to keep her face turned into his chest, but it was Aunt Evelyn who was speaking, her thin, handsome face immeasurably startled.

'I did knock, but no one seemed to hear me. What's happening here, Ingo? I saw the light.'

'What does it look like, Evvy?' Ingo said with his habitual mocking arrogance.

'In my day it was known as seduction.'

'I have to admit it was getting to that stage. What a good thing you arrived!'

'Genny?' Aunt Evelyn's voice trembled.

Genny didn't move, still brushed with the most exquisite violence.

'Don't worry, Ev,' Ingo said, 'she's all right, even if you've blasted all our dreams.'

'Dear child, shouldn't you come up with me now?'

'I'm trying to tell you, Ev, she's all right!'

'Shouldn't she be allowed a say?' Aunt Evelyn asked, mildly for her.

'She's trembling so much I don't think she can find her voice. Genny belongs to me, Ev. You know that!'

'Then I insist you marry her!'

Genny could feel the dark laughter start in him.

'I might love her above all else, but do you really think marriage, Ev?'

Something twisted near Genny's heart, like a sharp little knife. She put a hand up to her tumbled hair and Ingo looked at her, faintly smiling as she slipped the strap of her dress back on her shoulder. 'I wouldn't marry you if you were the last man in the world!' she said emotionally.

'Oh? I didn't think you'd go in for an open arrangement either. You know I like to put my brand on everything, Genny. Maybe you could change your name to Faulkner by deed poll!' She tried to pull away from him, but he pinned her wrists. 'You're beautiful, Genny. There's not another woman in the world I could look at after you.'

'Genny dear,' Aunt Evelyn said from the remote distrance, 'let me take you back to your room. I'm surprised you didn't think to defend your honour, dear!'

'Aren't you listening, Ev? She never lost it.'

'You stop laughing!' snapped Genny, fighting one hand free and making a swing at him.

'That's my girl!' he said, catching her hand and carrying it to his lips. 'I knew you hadn't forgotten how to retaliate.'

'Why did you ever come down, my dear?' Aunt Evelyn was asking worriedly. 'We all thought you'd gone to bed. Ingo wouldn't let me go to you.'

'I had a headache!' Genny said, looking so fragile and crushable and so wildly beautiful with her dark eyes enormous that Ingo suddenly swung up to his feet and cradled her like a ten-year-old. His dark face was curiously vivid, unpressured, almost carefree.

174

'All right, Evvy, seeing you've cast yourself in the role of duenna, lead the way, I'll put Genny in her own little bed and she can lock the door after me.'

'And that's just as it should be!' Aunt Evelyn said sternly. 'Really, the dresses you young girls wear! You do invite trouble. Shall I turn the light off here?'

'Please do!'

Evelyn turned and walked on ahead, thin and straight-shouldered, almost with a military bearing, lifting her magnificent Oriental robe as they went up the staircase. In Genny's bedroom Ingo put her down on the bed, and leaned over her to say with mock intensity:

'Sleep well, baby! You love me, I know!'

'Don't remind me!' She lay on her back, staring up at him.

'I'm never going to let you forget. But for dear old Evvy here, you'd have yielded entirely.'

'And you're going to hold that over me?'

'You seem to forget *I* never let you go. It was Ev who spoilt everything. Never mind, cherub. One of these days I'll get you all to myself, with no one to save you. Mine for the keeping!'

'Providing you don't have to marry me?' she queried.

'If we're going to consider the children, we just might have to!' he teased.

'Go away!' she said, covered in heat.

'If you two are really going to say goodnight, I think I'll go,' Aunt Evelyn said, an odd smile dispersing the clouds on her face. 'I'm feeling remarkably superfluous. Such a disturbing night all round!'

'What's so deadly about a fate worse than death, Ev? Genny isn't really cut out to be a spectator. She's a flame. Anyway, it was mutual and really an intensely private affair. You just happened to come along at the right time. I hardly touched her, when she literally sends me crazy!'

'In that case, Ingo dear, if you're to do this thing properly, offer the child nothing less than marriage. I know how you feel about Genny. I've always known.'

Genny sat up on the bed, the soft light that streamed around her deepening the colour of her eyes and her smoky blue dress, lightening her skin and her hair. 'I can't accept that I'm the only simpleton around here. I've always thought Ingo acted like a perfect demon towards me.'

Aunt Evelyn smiled. 'Really, dear! Do demons indulge small girls endlessly? I think he's been remarkably tolerant when you've delighted in being hurtful for years.'

'Thanks, Ev!' Ingo said carelessly. 'God knows you're the only one who defends me.'

'I love you, that's why, and so does Genny. Humour me and cut your goodnights to five minutes. I think I might sleep better now. You'll have to help me, Genny, with all the wedding arrangements. Felicity is worse than useless, but she'll never be able to walk down the aisle without the two of us.'

'Goodnight, Aunt Evelyn,' Genny said gratefully.

'Goodnight, my dear. You know, you've really taken a great deal off my mind!' At the door she turned and smiled at her nephew. 'You know, Ingo, I feel I have to tell you that you badly need to be loved by a woman like Genny.'

'But does she?' he inquired.

'It seems very much like it from where I was standing. I'm surprised you even asked.'

There was silence in the room for a moment after she had gone, then Ingo smiled with a shade of self-mockery. 'At this point I'm going to join you or move!'

She looked away from his handsome dark face. 'I

thought you were supposed to do what Aunt Evelyn said?'

'I can't for the life of me see why I should!' His brilliant gaze was slipping over her, the slender, singing line of her body, drawing her to him without even making a move.

She gave a little bewildered exclamation. 'You never say exactly what you mean, do you?'

'I'll tell you this much, I can't stand much more of this!' He leant over and dropped a quick, hard kiss on her mouth. 'Sleep well. I'm not likely to!'

'I love you,' she said as he walked away from her. 'I mean, I *really* love you.'

He smiled. 'Do you think I don't know that?'

'I want to hear you say you love me too!'

'Correction, baby, it's time you went to sleep.' He moved the door and when he turned around his expression was impossible to read. 'Take it easy with Flick tomorrow. She can't cope with too much serious-mindedness. I think she'll settle down with Dan. It will be difficult for her not to. He's not exactly what she thinks he is. In fact, when all the intoxicating excitement has worn off, Flick will find she's delivered herself to a real man!'

'May I invite Trish and Ian?' asked Genny.

'What an agreeable child you are! If you like, I don't have any real objections. Trish may have learnt a lesson. I doubt it, but at least she'll have the sense to behave.'

'I have this ridiculous idea she'll never like me!' Genny said, looking up at the domed canopy.

'Then you'll just have to understand.'

'It's not Trish I'm worried about. It's *you* I keep turning over and over in my mind. Maybe Evvy was deliverance at that!'

'Tell me about it one long dark night!' he returned neatly, smiling at her with his hard, mocking charm.

'That's more than you could ever dare to hope, Ingo Faulkner!' she said distractedly, becoming hopelessly confused about what he really intended to do with her.

'What a shame, when I've set my heart on it!' He was watching her with considerable deliberation, a very dominant man and a man who wielded too much power.

'You know, Ingo,' she said, flushing under that penetrating gaze, 'you're something of a villain. Don't think I don't know the difference between love and passion!'

'You can't have one without the other.'

'And you can't have me without marriage!'

'*Why* can't I?' he asked, his silver eyes sparkling.

'I'd die first. How does that affect you?'

His grin faded. 'Little idiot, you look hurt. Cut to the quick. When you're being so very serious, lost in that great bed, it's difficult not to give you an equally idiotic answer. Of course I'll get married, and when I'm ready to, I'll tell you!'

'Send me a telegram,' she retorted, 'I'm leaving as soon as Flick is married!'

'Good idea!' he said briefly. 'It will be a struggle keeping my hands off you otherwise!'

'If I were older ...'

'I could talk to you,' he cut in. 'As it is we keep getting caught in total obscurities!'

His voice was so dryly ironic that she moved suddenly off the bed, driven by some uncontrollable force.

'Don't go!'

He wheeled about, his silvery eyes flashing in his dark, forceful face. 'Can you see now why I don't let you make up your own mind?'

She stood there, her eyes clinging to him as if he were her only support. 'What's happening to me?'

'That's easy, but I can't do a thing about it at the

178

moment. Go to bed, cherub, you looked played out on your feet!'

'I never *meant* to feel this way about you!' She put her hands to her temples, visibly trembling, and burningly aware of him.

'You'd better do as I say,' he said in such an unsettling kind of voice that she had to fight out of her moment of crisis.

'Goodnight, Ingo!' she said like a weary, obedient child.

'It's all rather cruel, but necessary, baby. Goodnight!'

The brief ceremony was over and everyone, representing a wide cross-section of Faulkner relations and friends, seemed to be having quite a time for themselves with a free run of the house and the magnificent gardens. Dress was formal and all the women had been asked to wear flowers in their hair, so that the garden looked like a spring renaissance, with dresses of every colour and all the soft, summery materials. After a hectic and often onerous year in his legal office, Ian decided he wouldn't have missed it for the world: the pageant of beauty, the laughter and the conversation drifting thickly through the air, the atmosphere that belonged uniquely to Tandarro. He lifted his glass and emptied it, pleasure enveloping him and soothing his senses.

Flick was moving in and out among the guests, a dream in heavenly blue chiffon with a large picture hat weighed down with hand-made roses, while the whole scene was recorded for ever with a film load that seemed to Ian to go on for ever. Her new husband, Dan Howell, having survived the ceremony, was now laughing heartily and accepting congratulation and the accompanying slaps on the back. A fine-looking man, well over six feet, Ian supposed, he was thus able to take it.

There wasn't a man there who looked happier, and Ian decided maybe Felicity would find happiness and security after all. He sincerely hoped so, for he had always liked Genny's mother. She was really a fantastic-looking woman, seemingly ageless, with a double string of the most impeccable pearls, that she kept fingering sweetly, falling to her breast, with the beautiful diamond clasp turned sideways to be seen and not hidden beneath the filmy blue brim of her picture hat. They were Faulkner pearls, Trish had complained to him— Ingo's wedding present to his cousin. The diamond earrings and a ring big enough to trip over were the groom's very convincing declaration of love.

The children, dressed in brand new outfits, were mirroring their excitement, and had started to shout and run about the garden, so Trish had gone off to check them. He and Trish had arrived the previous day by taxi plane and the first critical moments were over. As soon as Trish could stop feeling jealous of Genny and taking little swipes at her in private, the happier Ian would be. He had always considered Genny a knockout, but maybe her kind of beauty didn't improve her relations with other women. Ian, who saw trouble every day in his profession, knew all about jealousy and its tiresome and often disastrous effects. His eyes followed his wife with a mixture of censure and approval. She looked beautiful in a three-tiered ruffled dress in a Florentine gold, her long black hair very fancifully coiffured, trailing a spray of tiny gold flowers down the back. She was acting as near to relaxed as he had seen her these past few weeks.

Unwillingly his mind was drawn to his mother-in-law. Poor Marianne! She was dying a little every day, consumed with the need to make her peace with her son. The tragedy of the whole business Ian had seen repeated many times in the divorce courts. He saw both sides; Marianne's and Ingo's, whom he admired tremendously. There was only one person who could ever get Ingo to change his mind, and Ian decided there and then that he wasn't going to listen to another word of criticism about her. Even Trish had been forced to admit that it had probably been Genny who had talked Ingo into letting them come. Whoever it was, and Ian was certain it had been Genny, he was very grateful. Tandarro was a miracle so far as he was concerned, a throwback to the romantic Colonial days, with the house so grand and the vast gardens. A kind of Outback Tara. An irresistible kind of place, and he surrendered himself to it every time.

The brilliant sunset was fading, a sensuous, spectacular affair that had bathed all their faces and garments in rose. Very soon the happy couple were expected to leave on the first leg of their trip back to America, stopping overnight in Adelaide before picking up their next flight the following day. Flick's fourth wedding it might have been, but no one seemed battle-hardened. Quite a few of the women guests had shed tears, including Trish, to Ian's surprise. Genny, in a heavy white silk with a white full-blown rose behind one ear, was trying valiantly not to show her finely wrought nerves.

Her beauty seemed heightened, if anything, by her undoubted heartache. She too was wearing some of the Faulkner jewellery, Trish had hissed at Ian: necklace and earrings in diamonds and Columbian emeralds, part of a four-piece set that had belonged to their great-grandmother, and if he didn't believe her he could go take a look at the portrait in the long gallery. Ian didn't consider that necessary. In fact he was familiar with the portrait and the necklace because he was an intensely observant man. It suited Genny beautifully, glowing and flashing against her golden-tanned skin and the low halter neckline. Trish in her quiet fury had evidently forgotten that Ingo had given her some beautiful pieces of family jewellery when they were married. If she rarely wore them, she *did* have them, and no cause for complaint. Ingo, in his complexity, had actually been very good to his mother and sister, but he was a man of strong feelings and his mother might as well reach for the moon as reach for him. Anyway, Ian had told Trish in the privacy of their bedroom, at the first sign of a tantrum from her he would get them all home and forgo his holiday altogether. It seemed to have had a most beneficial effect on her until she had seen the emeralds on Genny. After all, Genny wasn't getting married, she had whispered *sotto voce*, and Ingo spoilt her rotten.

By the time Felicity came downstairs in her going-away outfit, her face aglow with a fresh influx of youth, those who were able all grouped about the base of the stairway, spilling over into the entrance hall and the main drawing room. Felicity's sky-blue eyes focused on her daughter's face and she threw her bouquet with careful aim. Genny, feeling intensely off-balance, couldn't seem to seize the initiative, and it was left to Ingo, who stood directly behind her, to catch it and put the small, exquisite bouquet in her nerveless hands, more aware than anyone of Genny's total vulnerability.

Everyone laughed and clapped and succumbed to the usual comments; everyone except Genny who looked so beautiful and so untouchable, her huge dark eyes gazing at everyone without seeing them at all. In plain view of everyone, Ingo's hand came up to caress her nape, easing the tension out of her as though it little mattered to him if everyone had to make a bewildering adjustment in all their old thinking patterns and the relationship that existed between him and his young cousin.

The sheer intensity of his feelings seemed to be flash-

'You were too young to do anything else. A good enough reason!' he said dryly, his hand in her soft curls. 'I had to let you misinterpret your feelings. I've always known what mine were!'

'Then why didn't you tell Flick?'

'It will dawn on her somewhere over the South Pacific,' he assured her.

'Say you love me!' she said ardently. 'I want to hear you say it.'

'It's brilliant to be *able* to say it!' he said with some mockery. 'I love you, Genny. I always have and I always will, because that's the way I am.'

'Then can I ask something of you?' she said a little huskily, searching his dark face. 'Some time, not now, I know, but some time in the future, could you please make your peace with your mother? I think she's suffered enough. Please, Ingo, for me. I promise you I'll love you so much there'll be love spilling over everywhere. Please say you will!'

He looked away over her head, the resistance in him slow to relax, his shimmering eyes very beautiful but hard. 'You're asking a lot, Giannina.'

'You loved your mother once!'

'And if I did?'

'You can't leave her to spend to rest of her life in Purgatory.'

'Do you imagine that's what she's doing?' he challenged her, his head lifting imperiously in the way she knew well.

She nodded. 'I'm a woman and I love you too. I know exactly how your mother feels.'

'You'd best tell me about it.'

'Please, darling, *please*!'

He drew her into his arms and kissed her as though he couldn't stop himself, a little ruthless, bruising her soft mouth, moving her deeply but not relenting until she was exhausted with sweetness. 'Maybe the first christening!' he said dryly, lifting his dark head, his face full of a hard mocking charm.

'I'll keep you up to it,' she said, breathing rapidly as the colour raced under her skin, the silver tendrils of her hair clinging to her temples and cheeks.

'But it won't be for a long time,' he returned instantly. 'I want you all to myself. I can never get enough of you, and I've no intention of wasting much more time. It's impossible having you so close to me without having you with me all night. I want you there wherever I turn. I want to make you love me the way I love you!'

'Why don't you start now?' she asked, her lovely mouth indescribably tender. 'Having a wife is a big responsibility!'

'I think I can handle it.'

'Then let it be soon!' she whispered. 'I'm witless and lost wanting you!'

He bent his head sharply, his face mirroring the incomparable answering passion he felt for her, finding her mouth with a refined brutality that seemed so natural to her that she clung to him placating him until the knowledge of her total surrender came to him. Then he changed the quality of his deep caress to a strangely fiery tenderness. He barely lifted his mouth from hers.

'I'm sorry, darling, am I hurting you?'

'No!' she smiled at him.

'It's the long hunger I've felt for you. I love you!'

'I know you do. There was only one way I was ever meant to go—towards you.' Genny glanced up at the darkening sky, wildly excited. 'I suppose we'd better go home.'

'Yes, *home*!' he said with a beautiful possessive smile, and gathered her in under his shoulder and turned her towards the car.

Have you missed any of these best-selling Harlequin Romances?

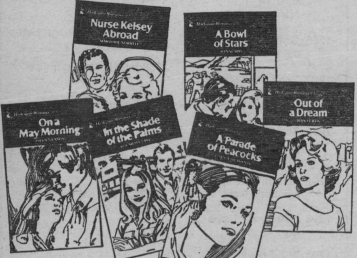

By popular demand... to help complete your collection of Harlequin Romances

50 titles listed on the following pages...

Harlequin Reissues